WITHDRAWN

The Party at Cranton

Books by JOHN W. ALDRIDGE

fiction

THE PARTY AT CRANTON

literary criticism

AFTER THE LOST GENERATION

IN SEARCH OF HERESY

edited works

CRITIQUES AND ESSAYS ON MODERN FICTION

DISCOVERY #1

SELECTED STORIES BY P. G. WODEHOUSE

The Party at Cranton

by

JOHN W. ALDRIDGE

DAVID McKAY COMPANY, INC.
New York

Once again
for
Leslie

The Party at Cranton

CHAPTER I

1.

AT ALMOST THE SAME INSTANT THAT THE gigantic howl rose in the room, Richard Waithe sensed its source and so remained for that instant the only person present not absolutely shocked out of his wits. He had in fact time enough while the others were registering surprise, dismay, and even something like panic—for when people came to a party at Cranton, they did not expect anything to happen—to let the thought touch his mind that, had he been one of those strenuously clever writers who begin novels with sentences like "Her face wore the mildly astonished look of an artificially inseminated cow," he would probably have said that the sound he had just heard was one he could easily imagine some abominable old bull of a pterodactyl making on the point of orgasm. For a moment he fascinated himself with the image of two immense and ungainly bodies, half bird and half reptile, heaving and staggering about in the dust of some endlessly twilit Jurassic plain, the male, his great skinny wings flapping crazily for balance, suddenly rearing like some goblin's conception of Pegasus in stud, then clamping down in teeth-grinning triumph upon his shuddering mate's scarious behind, his wild shriek for that second the loudest sound heard on earth since the first

3

thunderclap of Creation, then dying away in an echoing rattle among dry stones and empty canyons, the silence settling again, inscrutable and everlasting, quite as if passion had never been or would be, and no creature even at the dawn of time had ever loved.

In a way, although he rejected it almost at once, the image, for all its self-consciousness and forced ingenuity, was not hopelessly inappropriate to the matter at hand—or so, at any rate, it seemed to Waithe in his present state of somewhat heightened sensibility. For the howl which had just disturbed such peace as there was in the room had above all the character of a rape, a bullying, egomaniacal, even somehow sexual assertion on the part of Arthur Keith Buchanan of his imperiously taken-for-granted right to violate the privacy and the nerves of anyone and everyone who happened to be within hearing distance. It was not, as Waithe well knew, in any sense a right which had been granted out of friendship or respect, although there were grounds on which Buchanan, while alienating the one, might still be said to merit the other. It was simply a right which he had created for himself out of his own monstrous conceit and frustration, and which he indulged at random and quite without restraint whenever he felt the urge and was sure of his victims. It was also—and this Waithe was conscious of going to some length of tolerance to concede—what idiosyncratically remained to Buchanan of the great vitality which he had once possessed or was alleged to have possessed. It was a substitute and in a way a form of self-repayment for the loss of a certain power of authority, a certain quality of perhaps heroic protest or disdain which he could no longer afford—indeed, no longer had—to express except as a boorish explosion of noise and air. It was, perhaps a shade too dramatically, what was left to be

4

socially used of all that sharpness of intellectual line and tough-
ness of moral fiber with which, many years before, coming out
of the South like some symbol-breathing dragon, he had rather
awesomely made his name and because of which he was even
now frequently feared and hated but almost everywhere indulged. But even as he conceded this, Waithe knew that he
had put the case to himself much too simply, that Buchanan
was the sort of person to whom any concession was an im-
possibility, least of all the one Waithe was just then making,
more to his own ego than out of any spirit of fairness to
Buchanan. For the man was quite obviously there before him,
apparently in full possession of himself and all his powers, a
being to be reckoned with *in toto* or not at all. To do anything
less would not be to diminish or disparage or excuse him one
fraction. It would simply be to confess one's own shameful
impotence, one's craven sense of helpless outrage, before the
impeccable fact of his being quite magnificently and imperturbably there.

He was sitting a little apart from the rest of the room—a
position he habitually assumed and that Waithe knew was as
precisely and desperately strategic as the tight deployment of
troops around some beleaguered outpost of last defense. His
face still wore what was left of the faint, slyly mocking smile
with which he had just met and—apparently to his complete
satisfaction—conquered the shocked glances and nervous laughs
to which his sudden outburst had given rise. But now the
offended and violated—such of them at least who dared—had
turned their backs on him and retreated into their interrupted
conversations, from which superior air of shared insult they
from time to time gossiped fretfully but still warily down at
him like flushed magpies swooping at the head of an invading

5

cat. And seeing him there, suddenly and perhaps a bit forlornly bereft of the undivided attention of everyone in the
room, Waithe was struck for a second time in a few moments
by his own singular power of analogy. For Buchanan did look
quite distinctly like a cat, sitting there wearing his most gravely
self-infatuated paw-licking expression, the slight smile still
faintly curling the corners of his prim little dried prune of a
mouth, his small eyes over the tinily red-veined cheeks ever so
slightly lidded, his short, conservatively dressed body relaxed in
the chair, his daintily slender feet crossed before him, the inevitable glass of bourbon in one hand, the inevitable cigarette almost affectedly erect between the third and fourth fingers of the
other—so secure in his little kingdom of conceit. It occurred to
Waithe that the man positively radiated femininity, although
why the thought should come to him at this late date with the
charged portentousness of a detective intuiting the identity
of a murderer, he could not begin to imagine, unless it was
because he had assumed, at least until recently, that Buchanan
had no sex at all. Yet it was obvious that Buchanan's femininity, if such it was, was not the sort that could quite be exposed by a hearty clap on the shoulder and a triumphant
"Aha, I have found you out at last!" It was, in fact, if anything
just what accounted most for the really extraordinary mag-
netism which, whatever else might be said about him, Waithe
had to admit he possessed. For it was not the femininity of
the typical, over-cultivated, sensitive man in whom the demands of taste had drained sex down to a dry perversion. It
was, on the contrary, that strangely deceptive sort which
Waithe had so often observed in Southern men, the sort that
suggests not weakness or aridity but a kind of very strong, yet
delicately poised internal order and balance, a dynamic tension

6

of gracefully opposed sexual opposites, man-half and woman-half existing together in perfect harmony. It was almost as though, through some vastly clever form of genteel skulduggery, Southern men had managed to avoid service in the Hundred Years' War of nagging female attrition which had slowly forced their Northern brethren into the untenable position of aggressive single-sexedness, and from there into their strategic withdrawal into passive neither-sexedness. And even as Waithe allowed himself to admire the subtle justice of the impression —for, whatever the reason, Buchanan did indeed radiate—he became aware of the fact that others apparently shared it with him and, by so doing, confirmed its justice.

For Buchanan, whom Waithe only a moment before had had the sense of seeing rather forlornly abandoned by the room, was obviously anything but alone, although one might have judged from the expression on his face that he was securely at home gazing in solitary appreciation into his bathroom mirror. Scattered on the floor at his feet in various attitudes of rapt supplication—almost as though they had been brought there for sacrifice and had remained in spite of themselves to worship—were several of the more attractive younger faculty wives. At the moment that Waithe became conscious of them, some of the women were still giggling and whispering excitedly to one another over the man's outburst; others stared wide-eyedly up into his face with that demurely wondering look of little girls who have never before found themselves so fascinated by any man not their father; while still others were leaning back, stiff-elbowed, on their hands and simply letting the charm of the man radiate down upon them, the way they might have turned up their winter-pale faces to the life-giving sun.

7

At a little distance from the group, debarred from it, it almost seemed, by the invisible barricade of nearly devotional solemnity which Buchanan and his admirers had erected against the room, stood a young man whom Waithe knew to be the poet Anthony Marsh. Waithe was struck at once by the young man's highly uncharacteristic air of embarrassment, which seemed to Waithe as he watched to verge even more inexplicably on panic, for having seen Marsh in operation on many past occasions similar to this one, Waithe knew that, whatever else he might be (and on that Waithe could have written a close exegesis in two volumes), he was above all relaxed and thoroughly sure of himself in public. Marsh, in fact, after having launched his career in humble legitimacy entirely on his merits as a poet, obviously had made a special study of which of his personal assets served most to endear him to people, and had then earnestly set about developing them, quite rightly on the theory that endearing himself to people would get him much further in the end than any accomplishment he might be capable of as a poet. He had evidently decided that his most negotiable assets were gregariousness, a certain natural warmth, a faculty for occasionally saying something very witty, and a great capacity for laughing, without quite seeming to, at his own witticisms (he always seemed rather to be *sharing* the pleasure of others in his wit). Assiduous cultivation of these gifts had already won him a Rockefeller award, a Guggenheim fellowship, a scholarship for study in the Library of Congress, and a grant from the Fund for the Advancement of Poetry, on which he was now living. In time, perhaps because he had finally proved their absolute infallibility in getting him what he wanted, he ceased to make direct use of these gifts, and began putting on display whenever

8

he wanted to impress someone simply their surface manifesta-
tions, their outward forms and signatures, so that finally one
would see not the warmth and wit but the verbal-gymnastic
performance which had in the past always accompanied the
warmth and wit. A statement he was about to make—however
commonplace it might be—would invariably be preceded by
a kind of explosion and volcanic spewing forth from him of
great showers of sputtering "I means" and "I mean to says"
and "Don't you knows" and "That is to says," along with
choruses of burbles, choking gasps, giggles, and emphatic arm-
sweepings and finger-stabbings of the air. And his listeners,
like those famous conditioned dogs, would begin at once to
salivate their response, breaking delightedly into laughter, not
so much because he had managed to say anything funny—for
they could hear little or nothing of what he actually said—but
at the signal that he was launching into the performance
which had always accompanied his saying anything funny.

Marsh was apparently even now working up the courage to
initiate such a performance for the benefit of the man who sat
before him imperiously dispensing audience to his little court
of admirers. Waithe could easily imagine what his gambit
would be. It would take the form, if he knew Marsh, of some
fabulously esoteric literary question which he had been saving
up for days and polishing to such a high white brilliance that,
with luck, it could be counted on to sear into Buchanan's
brain an everlasting consciousness of Marsh's unimpeachable
merits. And Waithe was well aware of just how important
this was to Marsh, for not only was Buchanan one of the very
few people of influence whom he had not yet had the opportunity to impress, but Marsh's current fellowship was fast
running out, and he had thus far heard of no one who seemed

9

about to recommend him for another. Waithe also knew, and he knew that Marsh knew, that Buchanan had never read so much as a line of Marsh's poetry. But that scarcely mattered since it was well known that he had never read the work of any of the young men whom he had recommended for fellowships and prizes in the past. The choice was usually made—so Waithe had been told—on the basis of some chance or, as in Marsh's case, carefully calculated personal contact, and nearly always for reasons that could be traced to some sudden increase in Buchanan's normally limited supply of benevolence following on an inflation of his ego. On one occasion a coveted award had gone to a young novelist because he had remembered at a party that Buchanan drank bourbon instead of scotch. A young critic was similarly favored because he had had the simple good judgment and almost terrifying directness to compose a flattering critique of Buchanan's collected works. Another young man, a poet who, as it happened, had never published anything, was sent around the world and granted a stipend which enabled him to live and write comfortably in Paris for two years simply because at a dinner at which Buchanan was present the poet's wife had worn a very low-cut dress and served a remarkable shrimp soufflé. But Waithe had also heard of just as many cases where, for reasons as maddeningly mysterious as the others were banally transparent, none of these bribes had worked at all. Marsh, however, had apparently not heard of them, for it was something far more sanguinary than mere nervousness that shone in his face as he stood stiffly before Buchanan and in the next moment discovered the opening syllables of the speech that, for all he knew, might in one stroke establish his future as securely as any Frank Merriwell might have established his by speaking thoughtful words of simple kindness to a shabby old man who turned out to be an eccentric millionaire in disguise.

As Marsh stood there sputtering and gurgling, his wrinkled little elf's face twisted into the ghastliest of propitiatory grins, one hand ferociously sawing the air before him, the index finger stabbing down as if woodpeckering persuasion directly into Buchanan's skull, it seemed to Waithe that, with the element of surprise coupled with the sheer violence of the attack on his side, Marsh had distinctly won the initiative and was fast gaining ground. Great shuddering spasms of "I means," "Don't you knows," and "That is to says" were, in fact, erupting from him with such masterful intensity that some of the young wives, ever sensitive to the least shift in the balance of masculine power, were already turning away from Buchanan and beginning to favor Marsh with their anxious appraising stares. As for Buchanan himself, he sat rigidly through the first seconds of Marsh's assault as if paralyzed by a hammer blow, an odd red gleam of alarm showing dully in his eyes, one of his hands from moment to moment rising from the arm of his chair and falling back as though groping feebly for the strength to lift itself against the deluge of language. Then the light in his eyes appeared to flicker and change to a dirty yellow. Somewhere inside him the stalled traffic of sensation began to move, then it began to race, and in a single terrible flash of intuitive vision Waithe felt the sudden realization of his danger sweep over Buchanan, a realization that he was on the point of being disastrously outmaneuvered, that, in fact, a force of social fraudulence far superior to his own was even then rattling at his very gates, about to sack his position, rob him of all his plundered eminence, and shatter his sovereignty forever. His reaction was as

swift and convulsive as the closing of an eyelid before an on-
rushing gnat. With an immense heave he swelled out his chest,
sucked in his cheeks, threw back his head like a hound at the
moon, and let forth for a second time into the room his
gigantic howl.

The effect on the young wives was overpowering. For an instant they sat petrified like Trojan women receiving the news
of the slaughter at the Scaean gates. Then the tension snapped;
it almost seemed to Waithe that a sigh of something like passionate release rose from them; and they collapsed in joyous
hysterics, madly slapping their thighs, clasping their middles,
falling shrieking upon each other's necks. Across Marsh's extremely vacant face there slowly began to pass the possible
configurations of grief, terror, outrage, and nervous prostration.
He even appeared for a moment to be fighting the impulse to
rush from the room and dash out his brains. Then, finding
himself fixed by Buchanan's craftily appraising eyes, he hurriedly put on his most ingratiating expression and began with
precise political appropriateness to laugh.

2.

The difficulty, Waithe told himself—and the thought had
been struggling for formulation in his mind ever since he had
entered the room almost an hour before—the difficulty lay in
separating illusion—what one thought one saw—from the truth
that one was really witnessing. He had had an almost overpowering sense when he arrived at the party of walking
head-on into a cliché, one of the most suffocating clichés of
the time, and while the feeling was not exactly new to him—
since he had known seemingly forever that most of the ex-

periences of modern life had, in one way or another, already
been done to death—still, his sense of the degree to which this
particular experience had not merely been done to death but
battered in the process almost beyond recognition had this
time come to him with such depressing clarity that he had
wanted to run around flinging open windows in the wild hope
that some passing creature of the night would be tempted to
crawl in and startle the room into a semblance of originality.

He had begun to feel it from the moment when his smiling
hostess had met him at the door and had stood there absent-
mindedly clasping his hand while gazing steadily over his shoulder into the darkness—the deeply uncomfortable sensation
that it had all happened, or he had read about it all happening,
somewhere before. Then as he entered the room and stood,
feeling more than a little dissociated, among the urgently
chattering people, he realized that while it all unquestionably
had happened before and would go on happening many times
again, that fact made it no less true that, whether they were
aware of it or not—and Waithe had every reason to believe
that at least some of them were aware of it—the people in the
room were as neat a little collection of *dramatis personae* as
one could ever hope to find, all looking as though they had
just stepped out of or were about to step back into some terribly witty novel that was being written about them. At any
moment now they would begin behaving like the people in
those fashionable novels of academic manners such as the ones
by Miriam Hornblower and Lester Fleischmann who, Waithe
noticed, were at that very moment standing together smiling
and talking and very probably gathering material about each
other in a far corner of the room. Their novels were always full
of terribly recognizable people who went around doing things

that, except on one or two distinctly untypical occasions, Waithe had never seen anyone actually do—although the line between what he had seen and what he had read was fast blurring in his mind—things like making ponderous multilingual puns, or plotting the selection of the next president of some small, progressive girls' college that was invariably Sarah Lawrence, or getting drunk and having frantic sexual adventures in bathrooms. As Waithe contemplated the scene before him, he wondered in what transliterated version it would probably present itself to him at some future time in the pages of an as yet unwritten Hornblower or Fleischmann novel. On a sofa directly in front of him sat Dorothy Murchison, the visiting classics scholar in honor of whose just completed series of lectures the present party was being given. Dorothy was an extremely attractive, almost tritely neurotic woman whom Waithe had known even more tritely on terms of absolute intimacy for a period during the war years. At the moment she was leaning back displaying her very remarkable knees and idly studying the room over the rim of her cocktail glass. Three sociologists, whose names Waithe could never remember, were huddled in a manner suggestive of conspiracy just to the left of the baby grand piano on which the host, later on in the course of these evenings, normally did Tom Lehrer imitations. Anthony Marsh, who stood in a little circle of people in the very middle of the room, was evidently engaged in choking to death, while his audience—right on schedule as always—was beginning to laugh heartily over whatever it was he had not yet managed to say. A short distance beyond Marsh, in a clear space that gave Waithe the feeling that it had somehow been roped off, sat Arthur Keith Buchanan, already enthroned in his usual great-man fashion and earnestly talking down to the first of his young admirers to arrive, a girl who lay very nearly prostrate at his feet and stared up into his face as though it were frescoed on the ceiling of the Sistine Chapel.

By partially closing his eyes and letting them go just out of focus, so that everything before him grew dim and a trifle fuzzy at the edges, Waithe was able to see these figures in what he imagined to be the blurred perspective of the novels that Hornblower and Fleischmann would undoubtedly write about them. In that perspective the mundane reality of the room—its overpowering pedestrian dullness—would disappear, and all the people who were gathered in it now in their various attitudes of open boredom and polite inanity would be brought leaping into grotesque life and made to act out parts in the fantastic dumb show by which the Hornblower and Fleischmann kind of fiction, in striving to turn them into characters, would transform them into monsters. Dorothy Murchison would gulp down her cocktail, her fifth, rise from the sofa, wobble, and slowly begin taking off her clothes. The three sociologists, one of whom would have been covertly observing the Murchison knees for the previous half-hour, would also get up, down their drinks, and slink off, the one, with hot anticipatory eyes, toward the sofa, the other two toward the kitchen where, in various dark recesses formed by cupboards, laundry bins, and mop closets, the drunken faculty wives of Cranton University lurked waiting to be made. After battling mightily for the requisites of speech, Anthony Marsh would at last manage to choke out a terribly dirty story in medieval French. Miriam Hornblower or Lester Fleischmann (it all depended on which of them one read) would start making loud and brilliantly insulting remarks about the other; while Buchanan, the wild leer of a concupiscent cat spreading over his face, would suddenly lean over and begin grappling in the front of the girl's dress, at the same time muttering horrible obscenities in Sanscrit.

Such an approach to the scene was absurd, Waithe knew, a hopeless distortion of the real experience which, for better or worse, constituted the living body and form of the room and of the people in it. Still, he was forced to admit that it represented a considerable gain over the real experience when it came to action and drama. For all its absurdity it would at least contain something to catch the eye and hold the interest of a reader, and it managed to create a dramatic effect, however wildly bizarre, which was the effect real life had to be able at some level or other to create if the writer—even the Hornblower or Fleischmann kind of writer—was to make use of it at all. But what happened when real life ceased to create that effect, when the primary truth of it became its predictability, its dullness, its *lack* of overt action and drama? What happened when one found oneself inhabiting a society in which life had been so severely disinfected of passion and pain that all one ever encountered on its surfaces were the empty pretenses of people who, in losing passion and pain, had lost the means of human relationships? Obviously, one of two things happened: either one could exaggerate and distort real life, force dramatic interest, even sensational interest, upon it by falsifying one's picture of it into a Hornblower or Fleischmann parody; or—and this was the much harder thing —one could find some other, more honest and accurate way of making it dramatically interesting, while at the same time preserving the primary truth of its dullness and predictability.

Waithe had for a long time been aware—and the occasion of this party had served to remind him of it again—that the primary truth about the real life of Cranton was that, in the circumstances in which one was normally brought into contact with people there and had the chance to observe them (and that was almost solely at parties), very little ever actually occurred, very little, that is, that could rightly be taken as an indication of the true nature of the people or of the realities around which, during their extra-party hours, they presumably conducted their lives. Cranton parties were all a preparation for something that never happened. They were so strictly regulated by the rules of some complicated and secret code of etiquette that the people at them behaved as though they had all put on masks at the door and were engaged in playing a vastly esoteric game of charades. Yet because of what he knew —and in some cases it was a good deal more than he wanted to know—about their private histories and problems, Waithe was also aware that the lives of most of them were full of the materials of action and drama. It was just that, for reasons of convention which concealed deeper reasons of fear, insecurity, and generalized mistrust, no real connection existed between their party selves and their personal selves. The lives to which their personal selves belonged were pursued elsewhere and, it almost seemed, rather shamefully as if they were clandestine love-affairs, while to the parties they attended people brought only token-selves, little heavily ritualized *personae* under guard, which they used and put aside as soon as the time came to go home.

To write an accurate novel about them, therefore, as he himself rather than a Hornblower or a Fleischmann would do it, it would be necessary to portray these people in the situation in which one typically found them—that is, at parties doing nothing—and at the same time create for them out of what one knew of their backgrounds a personal life that would serve to fill the vacuum left by their party selves. This would amount to juxtaposing two views of them: one as they appeared in their normal party role, the other as the writer knew or could imagine them to be at those times when they took up the role of being human. But since one encountered them in life only at parties, one would have to be careful to depict them as *being* only at parties, or perhaps at one extended novel-length party, and then contrive some way of bringing in from behind, while still not disturbing, their essentially static party role, those elements of history and personality that would infuse them with dramatic life. The ironic possibilities in such an approach, the brilliant opportunity it gave the writer to play off, one against the other, the complex paradoxes latent in the conflict between appearance and reality, made a strong appeal to that part of Waithe's imagination which could work in sympathy with the writer's task. And as he stood, almost an hour after his arrival at the party, automatically sipping the cocktail that someone had given him and watching, while at the same time not quite seeing, what little went on in the room, he had already proceeded some distance toward visualizing the subtle effects which the scheme would be capable in the right hands of yielding up, when his thoughts were broken in upon by the sound of the gigantic howl that for the first time that evening rose abruptly in the room. Of all those present only Waithe remained unshocked by the sound, for, having heard it before on another occasion several weeks previously, he realized at once that it was Buchanan who had made it, a man about whom he felt he knew everything and nothing, before whom he stood in both awe and deep dislike, and whose image—perhaps because of these equivocal feelings—had always been associated in Waithe's mind with the paradox of Cranton life. So completely, in fact, had Waithe made this identification that it almost seemed to him that the man and Cranton shared the same secret, were even in some wild way conspiring together to elude, resist, or simply confound all love and understanding.

CHAPTER **II**

1.

ANTHONY MARSH WAS REPORTED TO HAVE SAID
on an occasion otherwise unmemorable that if Cranton had
not existed, someone would have been obliged to invent it.
The remark was generally considered to be one of his finer
efforts, and the fact of its being an effort—like all his attempts
at utterance—made it seem even finer. Almost on the strength
of it alone his reputation as a wit had been established, for,
since it was one of the very few things people could recall
ever having heard him distinctly say, they clung to it wonderingly and with a kind of secret triumph, as if they had panned
a nugget out of his rushing stream of incoherence, long after
the more accessible remarks of others had passed from their
minds. Waithe, however, never found it funny; he only
thought it accurate. It was undoubtedly true that the progress
of history, the lifting force of man's climb upward from the
jungles and swamps, had made the appearance of a Cranton at
this time and at some place in the world a scientific certainty.
It was even plausible to suppose that, as happened in the case
of all major contributions to the advancement of culture, the
powers of destiny would at the right moment have found an
inventor for it, had one failed to appear of his own accord.

But what disturbed Waithe was that, whereas others saw this as simply an amusing possibility, as something to joke about by way of suggesting that Cranton was too implausible to be quite true, he saw it as very nearly an accomplished fact. At least in that part of his mind which perceived intuitively and by "feel" the fundamental reality hidden at the heart of things, Waithe had always assumed that Cranton *had* been invented, and that the inventor was Arthur Keith Buchanan. Almost from the moment when he had first set eyes on the man, Waithe had been obsessed with the notion that in some unimaginable way the town had sprung fully blown from Buchanan's head on that fateful morning now more than a decade past when, newly dispossessed of his kingly province in the South, he had arrived there, his crown in his brief case, and at once decided that he would need for a realm something more commensurate with his talent for tyranny than simply a stagnant, mosquito-ridden swamp. The swamp had of course been eradicated—although the mosquitoes had not—over a hundred years before that morning, and the town had in the interval grown up in its place. But historical fact was not necessarily intuitive truth, and Waithe's intuition told him that his own view of what had occurred was much closer than history to the truth of his feelings about Cranton. The point was that he *saw* Buchanan there at the beginning, at the very dawn of Cranton history, and the image dramatized for him his persistent sense not only of the town's mysteriously spontaneous origins but of Buchanan as founding father and maker, the seminal appointee of destiny. Besides, in a certain real way Cranton had been a swamp, a cultural swamp, far more stagnant than the original one, before Buchanan came, and he had transformed it—or at least the part of it that

Waithe knew best—into a cultural oasis, if only so that there would exist somewhere in the world a creation of his perfect enough to justify his exalted opinion of himself. By so doing he had made the town unmistakably his own. It had become his Athens, or, since it had for him even more daughterly regard than any of the young admirers who sat at his feet, one might have called it his Athena. Certainly, one did not have to live in it very long to feel that it could have come into being only by a process of mental parturition. It was a place not only of the mind, and of Buchanan's mind, but, it almost seemed, altogether *in* the mind. It appeared to have only the most insubstantial existence as an actual town; its real existence was as an idea, a theory of life, a grandiose Platonic conception of the way things ought to be. It was what Buchanan would have constructed if he had been obliged to embody his own idealized image of himself in town form, and this—according at least to one report—was precisely what had occurred. He *had* been obliged. Years before, it was said, he had left behind the possibility of making himself over in the image of the man he had wanted to be, and so he had made Cranton in that image, or Cranton had made itself in the image of the man it thought he was. The town was his substitute for the successful creative life, just as he was the town's symbol of the successful literary life. But like all things that are achieved at the expense of something else, both Buchanan and Cranton were a little hollow and fraudulent, a little defective in their reception to life, a little deficient in the stuff of reality. One had the sense of too many swamps having been drained to produce them, and some had been swamps with live fish in them.

2.

Exactly which swamps and what variety of fish had gone into the sacrifice it took Waithe a very long time to learn, and when he finally did, the truth was not so much revealed to him as dredged up by his slow labor of excavation beneath the surfaces of the enigmatic life around him. It was almost as if, to get at the truth, he had been obliged imaginatively to dig down through history to the moment just before Cranton began, put back the swamps and restock them with fish, establish again on the spot where the town now stood the pristine Edenic condition of things, so that he would have some standard against which to measure what had been lost in bringing it to birth. For that was the whole point and difficulty. Something *had* been lost in the creation of Cranton, and to find out what that something was, one had to do more than simply see what was there before one. One had to see what was *not* there as well, be able to hold in the mind an image of what ought to be, or may once have been there. For on the surface Cranton was above all characterized by its absences, the empty hollows where the swamps and fish had been. Waithe's first impressions there had been of some acute vacancy at the heart of things, some subtle defect in the mechanism which made reality real and life alive, and for a long time he had felt like a detective having to re-enact a crime in order to determine whether anything had been stolen, whether, in fact, any crime had been committed. Then very gradually he became aware that what had been stolen had long since been replaced by something else. The swamps had been drained to give place to an idea, the idea on which the tight little intellectual world, which was the proud essence of Buchanan's Cranton, had been founded; and what had been drained off with the swamps was all the live humanity that could not be made to nourish the idea.

The idea originated of course with Buchanan, and it beautifully expressed those central concerns of his nature which had lost their power to find expression in any other way. The idea was, in fact, a perversion of his image of himself as he had once wanted to be, at the same time that it was the sole means by which something of that image could be salvaged from the wreck of his past and made to work to his social advantage. For in the same sense that Cranton could be said to have sprung from Buchanan's head, the idea behind Cranton could be said to rest upon a Buchanan-inspired theology of the head, a sternly ascetic belief in the absolute supremacy of the informed intelligence, not intelligence directed to some creative end such as the production of art, the enrichment of taste, or the refinement of the spirit, but intelligence divorced from all these things and valued in the abstract and for its own sake. At the parties which served Buchanan's little circle of friends and admirers as a substitute for community life it was repeatedly borne in upon Waithe that the question which hung over every head like the sword blade of some unspeakable disclosure was not—as it would have been in certain other Cranton circles —"Whom do you know?" but "What do you know, and how much?" The human question, "What are you, and how much?" was never asked, if only because the language did not exist in which an answer could be phrased. The human was one of the things which had been drained off with the swamps, was the principal *something else* at the expense of which Cranton had been created. Intelligence alone counted, but since it was intelligence cut off from its proper meaning and function and desired merely for itself, it had value only as an object put up for public display, as an article of mental attire that one wore to impress others and to win from them a certain momentary sense of personal status. But this kind of status was also, by its very nature, meaningless, for it existed only in the eyes of its possessor and those who had the illusion of conferring it, and it could be spent as social capital only in the official currency of the group, which, in the case of Buchanan's circle, took the form of academic gossip and shoptalk, themselves substitutes for the hard currency of the real life of the mind, the one currency in which intellectual status can have true value.

These facts seemed to Waithe to account in large measure for the odd promiscuity of Cranton social life, the almost frightening absence in the town of any basis on which genuine human relationships could be conducted. It was perfectly true that whenever people gathered together (and that was constantly), they gave every appearance of treating one another with friendliness and warmth, even at times with something like affection. Cranton, in fact, was popularly supposed to have established the practice, which soon became widespread throughout the country, of regarding the social kiss as the only form of greeting that could properly be exchanged by two persons, excepting of course men, once they had been introduced. But one did not have to observe them very long to realize that such displays were merely appearances, and that the people who indulged in them were only pantomiming the gestures of feeling, as if they were acting out parts in a ritual whose significance had been lost in antiquity. For the truth was that feeling in Cranton had long since dried out from beneath the forms which feeling had originally created for its expression, and now only the forms were left, to be observed ceremonially, perhaps even with a secret nostalgia, as imagistic renderings and talismans, the retained relics of a dead politics of the human situation.

It did not matter whether one attended a Cranton party every night for ten years or had been abroad ten years and suddenly returned: one was greeted in each case with the same show of professional cordiality, the same mechanical assurances that one was mechanically adored. Even if one saw the same people at parties night after night for those ten years, one got no nearer to them than one had been at the first party, and one could just as easily have never seen any of them again, had some catastrophe so violent as actually to disturb Cranton intervened to prevent it. Waithe was, in fact, regularly astounded by the ease with which people disappeared from the Cranton social scene, were forgotten, and almost at once replaced by other people. But since people in Cranton were merely instruments of diversion and relief from boredom, they were interchangeable: one was precisely as good as another, provided he was precisely as pleasant. Waithe had had this extravagantly impressed upon him very early in his Cranton career. At one of the first parties he had attended he had happened to meet a man he liked instantly and in whom he thought he had found a potentiality for lasting friendship. There had been a single remarkable evening during which the man had confided to Waithe the whole intimate story of his life, his hopes, his dreams, his successes, and his failures, and Waithe had listened, feeling touched and grateful. But the next time they met, the man had treated Waithe with no more friendliness than he would have accorded a complete stranger, not, it was obvious, out of any sense of embarrassment, but simply out of indifference, as if nothing had happened between them or the memory of it had somehow been erased. A short time later Waithe had had a strikingly similar experience with one of the Cranton women whom he had taken after a party rather precipitately but nonetheless passionately to bed. When he encountered her again on the following evening, she had greeted him pleasantly but with a certain vagueness, and had soon moved off to engage a visiting celebrity in a spirited discussion of Dylan Thomas.

Such experiences served to convince Waithe that, in the intervals between parties, the people of Cranton simply retreated into themselves and drew their psychic blinds, shutting out all memory of everything that had taken place at the last party and effectively sealing up their consciousnesses until the next. It was as if they themselves sensed in some dim way that their social lives were unreal, and their failure of memory was the index of their secret rejection of the fact. But social life, to seem real and memorable, had to be conducted on a basis of mutual trust, security, and equality. The whole of one's being had to be freely and openly tendered and received with grace and good will before the veneer of social anonymity could be penetrated and contact with reality made. But this could not happen in Cranton. Status, not communion, was what counted there, and the urge for it was a competitive, separating urge that converted people into ranked items on a perpetually changing balance sheet. Besides, the Cranton variety of status had its own special liaison with unreality. Intellectual eminence was ostensibly the one sure means of attaining it, but the difficulty was that, except for a few special cases like Buchanan, no one really knew who had eminence, least of all whether one had it oneself. Officially, of course, everyone who lived in Cranton, by the very fact that he lived there, was supposed to have some. But that simply meant that, to count for anything, one had to have a good deal more than other people had, or risk counting for nothing with only some. The great problem was to contrive some way of getting it in a situation where everybody had it and wanted more than you had and did not want you to have any.

At parties, therefore, a typical mannerism was a covert shifting of eyes in the person to whom one happened to be talking, a quick census-taking and grading of the competition around one, a secret effort to calculate whether one was really spending one's time in the very best company, or whether it might not be more politic to crash *that* circle, in which some-one seemed at the moment to be saying something really profound. No one could have told what being seen conversing with a particular group might possibly do for one. There was always a vague promise of job opportunities, invitations to lecture and review, offers of fellowships and seats on prize committees, but these were never very definite or often forth-coming. It was more that one had to get one's sense of impor-tance from somewhere, even if only by association or prox-imity, even if only through the company one kept or was kept by. Since one never knew exactly what or who would pay off, one had to be always on the alert and ready to exploit any opportunity that presented itself. But it sometimes seemed to Waithe that there were moments when he could detect be-hind it all a subtle suspicion, shared by everyone but acknowl-edged by none, that perhaps they were all victims of a monstrous self-perpetuated hoax, that perhaps no one really had status or could ever get it, that perhaps they were all in frantic pursuit of a goal that did not exist. At such moments

Waithe liked to imagine that he could actually sense a change in the party atmosphere, some slight stiffening in the carefully relaxed tone of things, as though everyone had been brought up short on the brink of a bottomless pit of conscience and suddenly assaulted by memories of the sacrifices dropped into it—the throats cut, the backs knifed, the reputations gelded— all possibly in the name of a lost cause, a phantom conspiracy. Then the illusion would vanish. There would be a flurry of nervous laughter, an anxious rattle of ice in drinks. The little gatherings of people—as restless as partitioning amoebae—would stir, divide, scatter, and re-form; individuals would detach themselves from one and drift to another, then drift on to the next. In the midst of it all, someone would venture a profound remark. Someone else, in spite of himself, would be impressed. Soon others would move in and surround the speaker like sidewalk onlookers at the scene of a fatal accident.

3.

This was the pattern of life in that part of the Cranton social world that Waithe knew best, a world whose hold on reality was so slight that it often seemed to him to exist only in his imagination. And indeed in a certain special sense this was true, for Waithe had never known anyone who felt as he did about Cranton or who saw it quite as he saw it. The Cranton he saw, therefore, was either something he imagined or something which, if one had the insight, was there to be seen: it was either the creation of fancy or the singular discovery of vision. But whichever it was, the result for Waithe was the same. He still saw something there that others did not see, and he was stuck with the fact. For better or worse, this was his Cranton. He had perceived it or created it out of his own head exactly as Buchanan had, or exactly as he had imagined Buchanan had; so in that respect it could even be said that he had created Buchanan, too. But both Buchanan and Cranton had an objective existence quite independent of Waithe: they were, after all, *there* whether he was or not. Each occupied space and moved inexorably through time with the rest of the wheeling universe. The problem for Waithe, however, was how to see them nakedly in their thereness without the intrusion of his fancy or his insight, either of which at once rendered the objective subjective, took Buchanan and Cranton out of their rightful, observable place in the universe and put them back into his head.

The solution that most often presented itself to Waithe, in the case of Cranton, was to construct a surrogate of himself, some immensely judicious but at the same time rigidly uncomplicated alter-intelligence, a sort of deputy Dr. Watson, who would be able to see the place without prejudice or distortion, insight or fancy, precisely as its image registered on the camera lens of his implacable brain. This proto-perceiver sometimes took the form in Waithe's mind of the classic traveler of old-fashioned fiction, the itinerant innocent and dupe, urban society's first man and victim, the sweating commercial with the tattered pack of hope and samples on his shoulder, who, very early on a certain spring morning in the year 19—, might have been seen, had anyone been abroad at that hour, trudging his weary way down the wide concrete road that ran straight as a dragoon's back from the wilds of Maine through the town of Cranton to the sea. Such a traveler, had he had the strength to lift his tired eyes, might have gazed upon a sight that would have gladdened the heart and enlivened the step of a less stolid man than this plodding Cortez, a vision of Cranton as no Waithe would or could have seen it, Cranton in all its clear reality, its plain unimpeachable thereness, exactly as it stood in the fresh light of the dawning day. At other moments Waithe projected a second figure of still more wondrous and antique simplicity, another first man and victim, this time of the American continent itself. This was a naked, starving Chingachnook and Ur-Buchanan, intrepid warrior and undisputed king of the wilderness, who, hunting down over the great plains and virgin forest lands to the south of Manhattan Island, might have paused one hot afternoon and stared with famished eyes out upon the swamp on whose vanquished bottom Cranton now stood, and caught there for a single breathless moment in contemplation of this miracle, this vision of a paradise of fish, may have wept and kissed the earth for joy and resolved to raise upon the spot a graven image of his god. But there were still other times when, giving way altogether to his penchant for reducing things to their simple unaffected heart, Waithe conjured up a final figure, the first man of all first men, the arch-victim-victimizer of Creation, old Adam himself, an uncertain, shuffling, mist-dimmed creature who may once have blundered, out of breath and out of time, upon a fetid swamp where gigantic reptiles lay steaming in the sun and, being dull of mind and weak of eye, he may have mistaken it for Eden and taken to wife a serpent and begotten upon the site of Cranton the knowledge of good and evil, man's first engaging act of love and, as history was later to prove, Cranton's last.

Whenever Waithe reached this point in his fantasies and began to feel the nudge of their evident absurdity, he always drew back, as though from the brink of madness, and forced his mind to address itself once more to the problem at hand. This time when he did so he realized that nothing could finally help him to see Cranton as it really was except his own powers of observation. He was, plainly and simply, stuck with them, just as he was stuck with the image of Cranton which they gave back to him. For all his imaginary *personae* had the common weakness of seeing, just as he did, only what their special bias or defect of vision allowed them to see. Cranton was a private image for them, too, an image which each of them carried in his head and which bore only the slightest resemblance to the real Cranton. Waithe saw it clearly as his task, therefore, to put Cranton together piece by piece in his own head, relying entirely on his own powers, exactly as he had so often observed it rising before him on the foundations of its swamp, its scholarly towers cold and proud in the blue light of fading day, the depths and heights of the human spirit —the bottom less than beast, the top somewhat more than man—oddly incarnate in a single place, one tiny point of earth where the forces of all time and history might easily be imagined to touch, join, and convulse together under the gathering night, along the sweeping arc of the world's passage among the stars.

4.

Waithe's impressions on approaching Cranton for the first time had been of descending quite precipitately into the fiery pit of hell. On that bright September morning now five years past he had driven with deliberate slowness down the broad highway out of New York, intending to regale himself with the sights and odors of the countryside and sharpen all his senses to that keen edge of excitation to which his mind had long since been brought by the prospect of seeing for the first time his new home. As a result, he dawdled along, heedless of the impatient traffic behind him, and took in with the easy pleasure of first discovery the changing scenery through which he passed. On his left at the very edge of the horizon he was just able to make out a far range of mountains tinted by a faint blue haze and already beginning to be touched at their upper slopes by the slight early colors of autumn. Directly below them, but a much shorter distance away, stretched the neat rows of orchards and long fields of what he took to be late corn, and nearer still there were pasture lands where cattle slowly grazed, and, bordering the highway itself, the regular square plots of truck gardens and a scattering of barns and houses. Then, so suddenly that it seemed to erupt out of the earth, there appeared on his right a scene of absolute desolation and waste. The land fell away from the highway into a vast gray plain that spread like a gigantic dirty plate clear to the western horizon. No shred of vegetation or sign of life showed on its surface, which had a glazed look as though the soil had been blasted by the heat wave of some ghastly cosmic disaster. But here and there rusty tracks ran beside heaps of smoldering refuse and ashes and glistening pools of black water, and beyond them over on the far edge of the plain, immense columns of heavy smoke belched into the thickening sky, against which, huddled dismally together like stranded conspirators from outer space, stood several dark forms which Waithe made out to be oil refineries and steel mills. From somewhere in the depths of these there rose up from time to time bright showers of sparks and bluish jets of flame, which —as Waithe was later to learn—lighted the night skies over Cranton with a continuous flickering glow suggestive of cities burning just beyond the horizon or the incessant stirring of infernal fires. A small river wandered brackishly among the refuse and ash heaps and, turning along the tracks, abruptly straightened and ran parallel to the highway, affording passing motorists an excellent view of its variegated contents. Its waters were a sickly chemical green, broken by darker patches of floating film and scum, and foul with garbage and the drainage of factories. On any day one might observe being borne on its flaccid current rotten planks, orange crates, old paint buckets (sometimes with the brushes still stuck in them), dixie cups, whole loaves of bread, eggshells, large and small tin cans, assorted articles of clothing, even an occasional rat—more asphyxiated than drowned—its tiny upturned claws clasped almost piously in death, its jagged mouth ever so slightly agape.

The scene reminded Waithe of Brueghel's "The Triumph of Death," if one could imagine it without the dense crowds of people and skeletons, with only the ravished landscape spreading to the sky and the smoke and flames rising in the far distance. It also reminded him—since he was, above all, a child of his age—of Fitzgerald's "valley of ashes." But the differences were significant and, to Waithe, disturbing. What Brueghel had thickly populated with humanity, Fitzgerald had seen merely in terms of a few miserable ash-gray men swarming with leaden spades up the sides of ash-gray cars. Both were striking images of desolation and death; but they were also progressive stages in the disappearance of the human, almost as though the threat—whatever it was—had gradually become abstract and generalized, had ceased to be explicitly *to* anyone in particular. Fitzgerald had already been dangerously symbolic. His scene had meaning only as it related ironically to Myrtle and Tom playing out their little drama of futility up in their sad sex-smelling apartment. Such awareness as Brueghel had had of the immediate, cataclysmic affliction by evil of whole masses of people, literally of the whole of stampeding humankind, had slowly been lost. And now there was nothing at all: no mad riot of people, no ash-gray men, no Myrtle and Tom, nobody to acknowledge the threat or to be afflicted. There was nothing now but the scene itself, empty and dead, as though the human had at last been successfully done away with under the new and entirely impersonal auspices of commerce. As Waithe drove past it, these thoughts followed one another in his mind, his car followed the highway, and the highway followed the river, until finally after several miles the outskirts of what proved to be Cranton came into view, the river ducked under a bridge and disappeared in the direction of the town, and a sign on the bridge informed Waithe that he was passing over Cranton River, the same that had once flowed cleanly and proudly, sparklingly cold and alive with fish, to nourish the swamp on whose site the town now stood.

It was Waithe's first view of Cranton as he drove into it that September morning that forever fixed in his mind the impression that the town had somehow been invented. He did not, of course, know Buchanan then and could not, therefore, have thought of anything quite so logical as the idea that the town had simply sprung fully blown from the man's head. But something of a very similar nature did occur to him, so similar, in fact, that it enabled him almost seriously to entertain that idea when later on he did think of it. For Cranton struck him at first glance as having the smugly superior air of a town that believed itself to have been immaculately conceived. Just to look at it was instantly to know that it could never have had anything so vulgar as a founding father (the only thing that later made the Buchanan idea acceptable to Waithe was the fact that it transferred the seat of fatherhood from the loins to the head). Cranton could only have been imposed from on high, decreed into being to the accompaniment of alleluias and seraphic trumpets, and populated on the spot with only those chosen few who, having known the Kingdom of Heaven, could be trusted not to settle for anything less on earth. One felt this, Waithe decided, not merely because Cranton had nothing to do with its environment—although it did not—but because the environment somehow appeared to have been warned to have nothing to do with Cranton. The environment had a thwarted, scared-off look, as though it had been startled in the act of trying to steal the town's virginity and had had the fear of God put into it. But, of course, it still hung around with a kind of slouching eagerness just outside the corporate limits and was obviously only waiting its chance to try again.

From all sides the most unspeakable reminders of the baseness of man and nature pressed themselves insinuatingly against Cranton's innocent outskirts. If one approached the town from the north, as Waithe had done, one came upon it as upon an oasis in a hateful desert and beheld it rising beyond the ash heaps and factory smoke like one of those fantastic meccas of the mysterious East, complete with minarets and palms, that one sees on packages of figs. If one approached it from the south, one passed through the closely neighboring town of Tankville, a sweaty jungle of industry where laid-off mill hands lounged against parking meters and stared at girls, and where at night the young in expensive financed sedans cruised the streets in search of mayhem. At the very gates of Cranton itself, standing in precise, uniform rows, as though set up by some giant idiot child who had received a box of them for Christmas, were the houses of new developments with names like Fairview Estates and Happy Hills. All the houses there were exactly alike, with picture windows that looked across to other picture windows, little lawns of thin new grass and raw earth, and front doors defaced by the kicks of children, the clawings of dogs, and the peeling of cheap paint. The way of life they badly housed was such an extravagant modern American cliché that the wisps of hair falling over the foreheads of young mothers as they stood at the stove boiling bottles actually were damp, and it seemed perfectly possible that the men really copulated with their automobiles and merely drove their wives. It was a place so completely and forlornly cut off from natural human community that the inhabitants were forced to create the illusion of one by a process of endless, automatic reproduction. Children there filled the vacuum left by the disappearance of roots, relatives, place, religion, handicraft—all the old barriers against the ego's naked loneliness in cultural space. But late at night, after the dishes were washed and the children put to bed and husbands and wives settled down in living rooms before the flickering, hypnotic light of TV, one knew that somewhere deep in their minds a kind of common dream did unite them all and give them for a little while a poignant sense of togetherness, the dream of one day being able to afford to move into Cranton and enter at last upon the Kingdom of the Chosen.

5.

By every known standard of scientific measurement, the citizens of Cranton were the happiest, healthiest, best educated, most prosperous, and most beautiful people in America. Statistics gathered over the years in carefully conducted surveys proved this, and Cranton had been so frequently the subject of surveys that the agencies which made them had long ago found it necessary to set up branch offices in the town. But one did not have to rely on statistics. One had only to walk down any Cranton street to see on every hand people so acutely and flawlessly perfect that at first glance one might not take them for people at all, but suppose them to be some sort of ingenious humanoid constructions put together by a cybernetics laboratory and being monitored around the block to see if they functioned properly. The young of Cranton, in particular, gave this impression. They appeared to belong to a wonderful new race so highly refined that all the old unsightly differences of feature, physique, and even sex had long since been removed from them through selective breeding. What remained was a kind of standardized sexual abstraction housed in a body that was the most agreeable compromise imaginable between male and female. If, as often happened on warm summer days in Cranton, one saw two of these beings approaching in tennis costume, one found it impossible to tell at any distance which was boy and which girl, whether, in fact, either was either. All one saw were two apparently identical, white-clad forms, both equipped with broad sturdy shoulders, brown symmetrical arms, and brown muscular legs. As they came nearer, one made out two faces, each as fresh and pretty as a girl's, as healthy and wholesome as a boy's, so strikingly

38

alike that one could easily have mistaken their owners for twins. It was only as one came up to them that one noticed that one of them had nice, small, perfect breasts, and the other a nice, big, perfect chest. Looking at them one felt as though the great American dream, which the rest of us had supposed long dead and in the grave, had, while we slept in cynicism, undergone a wondrous and, at the same time, wholly unassuming reincarnation. The rest of us, it became plain, had doubted and sneered, while Cranton, in whose dictionary the word doubt did not exist and upon whose serenely smiling face no sneer would ever have dared intrude, had marched quietly and happily on to victory.

The typical Cranton male—Waithe's own statistics ultimately revealed—was a four-martini, two-car man, father of three and a fraction, an Ivy League college graduate, and the owner of a home valued on today's market at not less than $35,000. He was about forty, of a little more than medium height, nicely built, with brown crew-cut hair gone slightly gray at the temples and tanned regular features set in a good-humored undergraduate face. At home he liked to wear very faded tan gabardines and very scuffed white bucks, and on hot summer days he went around town in brightly colored Madras shorts which showed off to perfection the well-muscled calves of his brown tennis player's legs. He was married to a blond woman who had once been remarkably pretty, but who now at thirty-five was only just very pretty. But, of course, she still had the figure with which she had been graduated from Radcliffe, and her face was the kind that keeps its youthful contours and tends with time to wrinkle rather than sag, so that she looked, and would go on looking, like an actress of twenty made up for a middle-aged part. Her vices were few and en-

tirely venial. Although she had had most of the usual opportunities, she had never practiced adultery, not so much because
of any positive desire to remain faithful to her husband, but
simply out of an absence of need. Besides, in her social circle
that sort of thing was considered rather passé and aberrant. It
was something one vaguely associated with a certain misdi-
rected bygone era and certain emotional problems which no
longer seemed quite real. If, therefore, a man had made a pass
at her, her immediate reaction would have been surprise, quickly
and almost apologetically followed by compassion, as though
she had not realized at first that the poor fellow was ill. She
did smoke a great deal, far more, in fact, than her husband,
and sometimes at parties she drank a few too many cocktails.
But her behavior was never visibly affected on these occasions,
except for a slight tendency to become more vocal about her
opinions—which she would expound in the peculiarly deep,
rather English voice of her class and type—and a certain faint
gleam of something a bit awesome that came and went in the
centers of her clear blue eyes. In the late afternoons of all
weekdays she could be seen at Cranton station sitting in her
old but excellently kept ranch wagon, her youngest child on
the seat beside her, a large Doberman standing up in the back,
waiting for her husband's train to come in. A few minutes
before it was due, she would look at herself in the rear-view
mirror, fuss with her hair, freshen her lipstick, and glance ex-
pectantly and with a look of real concern in the direction of
the tracks.

Her husband was not, as might have been supposed, what is
known in the current vocabulary of cultural types as an organization man, although he did commute to New York five days
a week and make $20,000 a year in the advertising business.

Nor was he other-directed, inner-directed, tradition-directed, company-oriented, executive-minded, a hidden persuader, or anything resembling what used to be called a Babbitt, a joiner, a booster, or a go-getter. He was rather the ideal embodiment of all that these types had aspired and failed to become before frustration had turned them into sour clichés. He was, in fact, the kind of achievement that in its perfection not only transcends clichés, but shames into impotence the powers of easy formulation that invent them. For the cliché had simply not been invented that could describe him, and if it ever were, he would quite effortlessly have rendered it obsolete before it could be applied. He was bright, logical, friendly, tolerant, quite suave and sophisticated, corrupted neither by materialism nor by money. Although some people might have taken him for a social snob, it was more that he was just unaware of those who did not live as he did, provided he had not taken a course in them at college. But he would have been quite capable of mixing on terms of perfect equality with members of all the various social classes. It was just that in Cranton he had never had the opportunity. The secret of his character was that he was a simple yet discriminating enjoyer of the good life in all its forms, the kind of tasteful happy liver in whom Cranton specialized and took most pride. All the poor benighted ancestors of his type—the bankrupt tycoons, the alcoholic bank presidents, the coronary Kiwanians—had worked themselves into an early grave to attain the goal which he so amiably represented. And if you had told him this, he would have looked quite serious, even solemn, and perhaps in an excess of feeling have sat down and written you a check.

There were in Cranton a great many facilities for the tasteful pursuit of the good life, so many in fact that the facilities for mere life had almost been crowded out of town, and one sometimes had to travel miles just to buy a nail to put up the Daumier in the bathroom. In the main street shops, the façades of which had been designed to give the effect of a London street in the reign of James I, one could buy woolens imported from Scotland, shirts imported from India, shoes imported from England, high-fidelity components imported from Germany, wines imported from France, the Rhineland, and South America, and foodstuffs imported from all over the world. One shop was given over exclusively to the sale of the materials of hors d'oeuvres. There one could obtain fillets of bear, whale, and rattlesnake, cans of salted Mexican worms and roasted Siberian ants, and the pickled eggs of a species of turtle found only in the mudbanks of the Upper Nile. Other shops, catering to those who were burdened by the feeling that they *had* everything, stocked only *objets d'art* whose authenticity as antiques was conjectural, paintings which may or may not have been the work of masters, and articles of furniture that looked like period copies but were actually genuine period pieces. The same sort of taste governed the purchase of such standard commodities as houses and automobiles. One of the most admired and sought-after showplaces in Cranton was a house which *looked* as though it had been prefabricated of parts left over from the construction of Levittown, but which had really been designed in a whimsical moment by Frank Lloyd Wright as a parody of a house such as Frank Lloyd Wright might have designed if he had been trying to design one as much as possible like those of Levittown. It gave every appearance of having cost around $13,000 to build, but of course everyone in Cranton knew that it had cost at least six times that and was the only house of its kind in the world.

As for automobiles, it could be flatly stated that the only Cadillacs ever seen on the streets of Cranton were ones that were passing through on their way to Tankville. All true Crantonians drove foreign cars, the smaller the better, or American ranch wagons, the older the better. But here again important distinctions were made. One did not drive a car *because* it was foreign and small or old. One could not, in making the selection, have gone through any of the conscious convolutions of thought by which snobbery had frozen up the powers of choice of the rest of America. One had to have arrived at it solely by instinct and the whispered dictates of good breeding. One had to have *known*, in the same way that one knew which fork to use when eating snails, that it was the only selection possible. In the preservation of such taste the commercial world of Cranton fully co-operated. Among the merchants there was no question of competing for the consumer's business, just as in the consumer there was no question of choosing among the merchants. As in everything else, Cranton had succeeded in evolving through the various perplexities of American commercial enterprise and in coming out the other end, the top end. The shops of Cranton simply stocked the best of whatever there was to be had, and the people of Cranton simply bought whatever there was that was best. If the horn of plenty had been emptied upon Cranton and its contents scattered all over the main street, no one would have moved to pick anything up unless it had a label showing that it had come from S. S. Pierce.

6.

In one respect only had Fortune been unkind to Cranton. Out on the farthermost western extremity of town, as far removed from its fastidious center as the laws of hydrodynamics would allow, ran the river that bore on its surface in the proud name of Cranton the effluvial discharges of the factories and garbage dumps located at the town's northern approaches. In the beginning, under the original dispensation of nature, it had flowed directly into the spot where the town now stood and performed the service of nourishing the swamp which had once been there. But after the swamp had been drained, the town established, the factories built, and the garbage dumps acquired, its course had been diverted, and so judiciously that it afterward seemed to belong geographically to Tankville rather than to Cranton. Cranton nonetheless remained, in spite of the most expensive efforts of modern engineering science, the chief recipient of the complex odors that rose on hot summer nights from its multifarious cargoes, as well as the most convenient source of provender for the swarms of gigantic mosquitoes that bred in the rank pools left by its seasonal floodings.

At a point on the river almost exactly midway between Cranton and Tankville stood a settlement of dwellings that looked as though it had been left behind in a sullen moment by the road company of *Porgy and Bess*. Here in casual circumstances of stagey squalor lived assorted Negro families whose forebears, it was said, had been brought North in the early days of Cranton University to act as body servants to wealthy Southern students. Their shacks, propped up on poles almost at the water's edge, were wretched plank and tar-paper affairs with low sagging porches, cardboard-covered windows, and long lines of perpetually drying wash strung between trees above the patches of stubbly ground behind them. By day the smells of cooking turnip greens and frying ham hung over them and gave a faintly inviting domestic tone to the unbridled stenches of the river, and at night there issued from their steamy, lamp-lit interiors a sensuous medley of laughs, giggles, and shrieks that blended disharmoniously with the serene chuckles made by the river as it ferried past their doors its little flotillas of garbage and scum. Through the warm days of summer ragged, grinning pickaninnies played in the moist earth beneath the unsteady porches; old hound dogs dozed and sighed in the cool of deep, scratched-out burrows; fat hens pecked and clucked among the children and dogs; fat women stood in doorways and gossiped from shack to shack; and men with black, shiny faces came and went in rowboats to scavenge in the river's bounteous currents.

It was altogether such a scene of exquisite typicalness as no investment of money or staging genius could thinkably have achieved, a Catfish Alley that outdid all Catfish Alleys simply because it was real, and real in a way that cut through and vanquished prototype and shamed into stammering obsequiousness the very idea of cliché. To contemplate it was to fumigate the doubting mind with images of a younger, cleaner, truer, and more fully human world, a world of bayous and deltas and rich, loamy plantation acres, of passionately singing voices and lithely laboring bodies, of lustful love in the sweet hot hay of noon—of the whole radiant vitality of a simple race working together as one people in tune with the immutable rhythms of nature and life. Yet like all things that appear to have escaped by some miracle the insidious erodings of time, it concealed in its heart a tiny spot of disease, one small but malignant symptom of fate's certain vengeance. For the truth unfortunately was that it was all a lie and a cheat, a huge practical joke played on the innocent trusting eye, a cold-blooded piece of drama-turgy done, as it were, with mirrors, false fronts, and dangled puppets, a conspired shoring up of fragments against an illusion's ruin, or—to put the matter in the most charitable light —a desperate shoring up of an illusion's ruin against fragmentation. It was all, plainly and simply, a creation, not of Broadway money and skill, but of aggressive senile nostalgia strugging to keep alive against the overwhelming fact of change.

The quaint settlement by the river was a production staged and directed by the oldest residents as a kind of Dearborn Village of the Negro race. It dramatized their most cherished vision of an ancestral past lived out in a long-ago lost Eden of a South they never knew but that was all they knew, and that had, as they advanced in years, become narrowed down in their minds to an image of a fairy tale, mosses and old manse kind of Old People's Home of a Virginia Creepered Paradise where, in payment for a lifetime of faithful service, one was pampered and nursed, listened to and consoled, by devoted white folks, but where at all times the Negro knew and loved his place. The settlement was what they had managed to gather together of the raw materials out of which they thought their vision had originated. It was as much as the modern world was capable of serving up as the materials of such a vision, and since they could not know that it was the hoariest of clichés and vastly inaccurate besides, they made do with it with a vengeance and defended it with a passion akin to madness against the opposition which, of course, they encountered on every hand. Sometimes at night, when passion got the better of the play, the giggles and laughs that were scheduled to issue from

46

the shacks would be drowned by sounds of violent discord as the old people made war on the recalcitrance of the young and instructed them, under threat of the fiercest forms of duress, in the principle that the show must at all costs go on. Some of the young had, to be sure, managed to escape. A few of the more intrepid males had stolen away from the river in the gray hours before dawn and found freedom in the neutral territory of Cranton by working as filling-station attendants and bus boys in fraternity dining rooms. The best of these had even contrived in time to become doctors, lawyers, and fairly prosperous businessmen in the Negro districts of Tankville, but even there the histrionic infection in their blood continued to direct their destinies. Like creatures impelled by a curse operating through remote control, they bought ranch houses in a Tankville new development, traded their secondhand Buicks for secondhand Cadillacs, their radios for television sets, their home brew for rum and ginger ale, and settled somnolently down to a parody of the habits of their distant Cranton neighbors that was even wider of the mark than the one from which they had escaped.

The old people meanwhile remained in rigorous command of the river tableau and of the services of their more obedient offspring. Behind the innocently rustic façades of the shacks, they bickered and cajoled, browbeat and threatened, but they managed through it all to hold their performers to the high standard their nostalgia demanded. The younger women hated the river, but they continued to live beside it. They thought their children were growing up like animals, but their children continued to play and grin among the dogs and hens beneath the porches. The men did not think it was healthy for them to be going out on the river in the boats, but they continued to go. Life proceeded as it always had, in a dimension out of time and beneath history, and buoyed up on its tranquil current, secure in a world they had quite deliberately made, the old went on with the pursuit of their concocted ancestral destiny. The women vied with one another to take in washing, scrub floors, and finagle jobs serving the children of better Cranton families in the capacity of mammies. On almost any sunny afternoon they could be seen stumping triumphantly along the quiet residential streets of the town in old, high-top shoes, their heads done up in bright bandannas, snuff sticks protruding from their gnarly old mouths, clutching the hands of nicely dressed little white boys and girls and mumbling self-consciously to themselves. The old men made a special point of gardening and doing odd jobs for these same families and of insisting over all embarrassed protests on addressing their employers, hat in hand, as "Cap'n" or "Cunn'l" or, if they were very old and had white wooly hair, as "Marse."

Sometimes on warm summer evenings after the day's work was done, the old people would give a benefit performance, the benefit being of course entirely to themselves. They would gather their families around them on the rickety porches; the old men would softly strum their battered old guitars; and all would lift their voices in songs out of their ancestral past, sad darky ballads, chain-gang laments, blues and spirituals that spoke mournfully of the suffering and loneliness of their race and of their own isolation so far from home in the white man's North. And sometimes rich landed Crantonians, seated in the cool of their terraces sipping their gin-and-tonics, would listen and nod and close their eyes and—as it was intended that they should—imagine themselves in the South of a hundred years ago, dozing on the wide magnolia-scented verandas of great, high-columned Virginia mansions, mint juleps in hand, and being serenaded by the sweet melancholy music of their loving, faithful slaves. It was an understandable enough fantasy on hot Cranton evenings, and who among Negroes or whites could have said that it had not been just that way in that far-off brother time, the only other time in history when such perfection as now reigned in Cranton had existed on this continent and for one long golden moment had lavished its riches upon two equally chosen races of beings?

CHAPTER III

1.

WHENEVER WAITHE TRIED TO SEE CRANTON EX-
actly as it was, he was always brought up short against the fact
of his equivocal feelings toward both the town and Arthur
Keith Buchanan. The two were inextricably linked in his mind,
pulled together, it almost seemed, by some haywire magnetiz-
ing faculty of the imagination that recognized, quite independ-
ently of him, that both were made of the same metal and so
could not resist the lure of molecular attraction. The one even
appeared in some altogether improbable way to be the issue of
the other, Cranton to be born of Buchanan, and Waithe could
not look upon the child without being troubled by its uncanny
resemblance to the father. The truth was that he both liked
and disliked Cranton, as he both admired and hated Buchanan.
But at the same time he knew down in the scrupulously audit-
ing division of his conscience that the dislike was the perilous
other side of near fascination, and the hatred a warily reversed
form of something that was almost love. He also knew that his
self-righteous concern for the genuine, which had caused him
to see Cranton in such a harsh, inquisitorial light, was his way
of sealing himself off from seduction by all that in Cranton
secretly appealed to him but that he consciously recognized

as false. He was himself one of the strongest tempted by the sins of those he condemned, and this moral doubleness, which became a doubleness of vision, was his flaw. But it was just as surely—like the suppressed lust of a Baptist missionary—his daemon. It gave him the motive power to care enough to try to see in the first place, for if he had been merely repelled, he would not have bothered even to look, and if he had been merely attracted, he would just have succumbed. The flaw of his doubleness made his vision possible. In respect to Cranton at least, he would have been blind without it. He *saw* the town as he did only because he could not make up his mind about it, and so was forced in desperation to do the self-protective thing, to gather up out of the whole range of possibility a single unflattering impression and lay it hastily upon the cold altar of his conscience, in order to palliate his secret attraction to the place and sanctify his dislike of it. But with Buchanan it was another matter altogether. Buchanan simply would not stay *seen*. No single impression, regardless of how unflattering, would serve to explain him, because no single impression was possible. Buchanan actually was in life an equivocal, protean figure, a double if not triple or quadruple man, and a man, furthermore, in whom equivocalness and doubleness had become professionalized into a social gambit, a way of maintaining his hold upon, his power over, others. He exploited unpredictability with all the deadly charm of a poisonous snake. He kept people constantly off-guard, hence, constantly afraid of him, because no one ever knew what form he would coil himself into next and when or if he would decide to strike. He had a dozen roles that he would capriciously and quite pointlessly assume, roles that ranged in character from saintly sweetness to infantile pettiness to wise-old-uncle serenity to drunken boorishness to unspeakable vulgarity, and sometimes when the histrionic mood was on him he would assume five or six of them in quick succession in a single evening, as if to prove how versatile he was at not being himself. He was a one-man amorality play who acted all the parts and then went out and browbeat the audience into applause, a horrible old ham who stole every scene he appeared in even though he always appeared alone. He affronted the world with a clownish disarray of incongruous shocks—deliberately outrageous *faux pas* and *non sequiturs*, unbelievable brilliances, unforgivable nastinesses, unforgettable greatnesses, immeasurable largenesses and smallnesses of mind and heart—and no one could have told whether beneath the grease paint he laughed or cried. The remarkable thing was that people put up with it, but it was not really so remarkable when one considered that they had no choice and would have been afraid to use it if they had. For above all Buchanan represented power, not any particular power, just power; his very act of calculated unpredictability had become symbolic of the indefinite nature of his power; and power in intellectual Cranton was what there was instead of heroism. He was an image of power so terrifying that there was literally no limit to what people would let him get away with. Waithe had seen him humiliate, insult, badger, vilify, and utterly destroy without rousing so much as a whimper in his victims; on the contrary, they seemed strangely flattered and grateful, as if even abuse coming from Buchanan constituted priceless evidence of the fact that in his eyes they at least existed.

How all this came to be, Waithe had no very clear idea, nor could he have told with any degree of precision where the real Buchanan left off and the fraud began, whether in fact, since the fraud was so skillfully perpetrated, there was or ever had been a real Buchanan. Like Cranton, Buchanan to Waithe was a series of blurred still-life sketches and light-struck snapshots, of startling quick changes and elaborate disguises, and he had finally had to be content to see them both just as they offered themselves in their public roles, their composed outer forms, simply as they registered for the moment on the touring eye of his imagination before whirling off into whatever void it was where they kept their real identities. Still, in Buchanan's case there was the abiding fascination of the human, the tantalizing possibility of one day being able to penetrate beneath the masks and disguises and glimpse at last the fatal secret, the mystic cipher graven on the tomb of a king embalmed at the bottom of all the excavated levels, the Troys upon Troys, under Troy-Buchanan, or perhaps a heap of dusty fragments, the broken icons of an illusion's ruin, or perhaps only a scattering of silt turned up by a digger's spade out of a great swamp's bed dry for three thousand years.

2.

The problem of excavating Buchanan, of digging imaginatively down beneath the many levels of his fraudulence until one struck one's spade at last upon the treasure or coffin of his truth, was complicated for Waithe by the fact that, unlike Cranton, Buchanan appeared never to have had a pristine Edenic condition. The town had seemed to Waithe ultimately reducible back to its swampish origins, to the primal moment of its initiation into life. But the swamp had, in Buchanan's case, been too thoroughly drained, and all traces of it so cleverly obliterated that the man stood before Waithe in an eternal present, locked into the present, it almost seemed, by the incessant, renewing variety of the roles he played. No past could conceivably be imagined for him; he could not be translated into any earlier or simpler state than the one he now occupied; he appeared never to have been born, always to be giving birth to himself or another of his several selves, always to be engaged in some perversely private ritual of self-bafflement. For all Waithe knew, he might very well once have been old Adam himself, but Adam expelled and incognito he had so resolutely become that one now saw only the masked outlaw in flight from his crime, an Adam perhaps of some fatal last day who had taken upon his own head the guilt of both his rejected Eve and Cain, the sin of the first venal temptation and the sin of forever murdering the brother of his real and secret self. The truth about him—if such there had ever been— had not lain inert and discoverable like some founding father's cornerstone at the bottom of his being. It had instead been slowly worked upon by the transforming pressures of time and conscience until it had finally become the driving energy behind the man he now pretended to be. Buchanan had used up the truth of his past to create the camouflaging fraudulence which was his escape from the past. The whole of his present being was a conspiracy against himself and the world. The enigma of his ever-changing roles was a means of keeping himself and the world in the dark as to the secret of his identity, the real truth about the man he once almost was.

Of all Buchanan's roles the two most familiar to Waithe were those of sullen silence and endless loquacity, the extreme forms of his effort to achieve self-isolation through a calculated derangement of the proper meaning of speech. Waithe had seen him sit utterly wordless for hours at parties, absolutely immobilized in the privileged comfort of his hostess's best chair, a plump, dapper, magisterial, little sphinx play-acting the part of a one-man bottomless pit caved in on itself, without one glimmer of light showing anywhere through the rubble of his conceit. He was so defiantly and imperturbably out of touch on such occasions that if a telephone had been installed in his brain, one could have rung him up endlessly and not even have heard a busy signal. Intrepid people had been known to plant themselves squarely in front of his chair and fire all manner of direct questions into him, only to have him turn on the steeliest of his bulletproof stares and perhaps grunt or huffle out at them from somewhere within the tongue-less obscurity of his being. At other times he would assume his seat of honor, and no sooner settled, cigarette-ed, and bourbon-ed than he would unleash an interminable, half-incoherent monologue, a kind of berserk valedictory address in which he would harangue his audience for whole evenings on every subject under the sun, with the countless trivial facts that had won him top grades in the class, almost obscenely showing off his knowledge like some dirty old man practicing intellectual exhibitionism on a public park bench of the mind. At such moments one could learn from him all about the spawning habits of a certain rare variety of Georgia fruit fly, the care and cultivation of sweet potatoes, the origin of the labial vocables in the language of Micronesia, the best way to cook mud turtle and where it characteristically lays its eggs, the medieval science of falconry, the philosophy of Montaigne, the proper form for the celebration of the Black Mass, the worship of Yemanjá, the esoteric sex cults of Bombay and Karachi, the acts of martyrdom of the various saints of the

Church, and the most substantial writings of Lao-tse, Labiche, and Pliny the Younger.

But in spite of the fact that it came to one under the auspices of a performance almost inconceivably brilliant, it was a sterile, oddly irrelevant kind of learning. For behind the performance Buchanan was obviously a man talking hysterically to himself, a man deathly afraid of talking to others for fear they might hear him, just as others were afraid of talking to him for fear he might not, might simply refuse to, hear them. He appeared never to have known what the rules of true learning were, but more than anything he seemed to want to prosper and gain authority in the learned world. In his anxiety to be accepted into that world, whose requirements for admission he imagined to be preposterously high, he had broken all the rules by outrageously exceeding them and, in the process, devaluating nearly to zero the intellectual credentials of just about everyone whose grudging approval he had hoped one day to be able to win. In his fear of flunking out, he had come dangerously close to flunking out all his teachers. And now he was left—although he did not appear to know it —with no one to compete with. The others had slunk away, and he was alone in the classroom, a babbling, frightened monster-schoolboy mechanically reciting his letter-perfect lessons to masters who had long ago ceased to follow or to care what he was saying.

Yet for all that, he was an indulged monster. No one bore him any ill-will whatever. He was, in fact, made over and deferred to on every hand, for the citizens of the learned world knew that they had in a way been responsible for his becoming what he was. He was the extreme form of everything they had aspired and failed to become, and they had after all made the rules by which his success and their failure had to be measured. He therefore became their object lesson and case-in-point, as much their victim as their god. He was a self-appointed, anxiously tendered hostage to their collective conscience, and so they pampered and petted him as though he were an idiot child or a misshapen mutant or the pitiful product of some regrettable weak moment of youthful folly. But through it all he remained unappeased, still insecure about what he knew; about whether he knew enough, too obsessed with his sense of inferiority to realize that he was so far out ahead of the competition that he was at last not merely deliberately but quite literally alone, safe in that final silence which was the ultimate condition of the success he sought, the silence that could be broken only when he chose to break it, by the sound of his own voice monotonously telling over the catechism which he had always supposed would eventually get him into Heaven.

3.

Inevitably, of course, there had to exist somewhere in the world an institutional equivalent of this silence, this supreme isolated success. There had to be some place where the sound of Buchanan's voice could be made to fall on ears even more exquisitely captive than those of his merely social audience, and where his power, instead of being scattered thinly at the feet of his almost peers, could be discharged in force at the heads of his complete inferiors. Buchanan therefore adopted the expedient which in Waithe's fanciful view had served him so well in the case of Cranton: he simply got himself pregnant by the right authorities and sat down and gave birth to a literary magazine. He christened it *The Cranton*

Review, and after soliciting sufficient funds from these same authorities to insure its proper start in life, he proclaimed himself its only begetter and chief editor, quite as if he had got it in a test tube direct from the loins of Fate. It was from the beginning a tiresomely pompous, overbearing little braggart of a review, the spitting image of its parent. In earliest infancy it showed symptoms of having inherited the family disease of acute oral narcissism, and since it was far more heavily endowed than subscribed to, it could afford to make a career out of talking to itself—which it thenceforth did. Buchanan had managed to wangle for it offices befitting its lingual capacities in one of the loftiest towers of Cranton University, and from there it trumpeted grandly down upon the literary world its muezzin cries of self-praise. There also, in spacious rooms paneled in the oldest and richest of mahoganies, Buchanan held editorial court and acted out the most ambitious and demanding role of his histrionic career, that of godhead or, at the very least, head god, appropriately enthroned at a point as close to Heaven as Cranton architecture could provide.

One had the sense on entering his presence of coming face to face with a hugely complicated intellectual switchboard of obscure circuits and plugged-in connections reaching out to the farthest-flung precincts of the literary universe. Buchanan dictating letters or shouting into his twin telephones was like some cosmic stockbroker-ghoul buying and selling shares on the cadaver market of other people's brains. At a word from him the reputations of lifetimes seemed to soar or go smash, whole empires of talent to rise and fall, and one could almost hear the chatter of a little ticker-tape machine reeling off yards of ominous quotations such as "Anaconda Trilling up two points," "American Tate à Tate down four,"

"Consolidated Kenyon and Ransom closing at 14.22." It was probably not true, as some of his critics said, that Buchanan had a direct line to the Nobel Prize Committee, and that they used to call him up whenever they were stuck for a decision. But it was true that the editorials which he regularly ran in the review, and which appeared to be written in some unknown foreign tongue, were in reality cryptogrammic aptitude tests, the solutions to which carried very great weight with the Guggenheim Foundation. Waithe had himself once solved one, showed his findings to Buchanan, and scarcely a month later found himself aboard a ship bound for the Orient with papers in his pocket entitling him to a year's research into the quality of early Japanese translations of James Joyce's *Ulysses*.

Buchanan kept about him in the review offices, to bring him cigarettes and to do his minor spying for him, an assorted company of heavily bespectacled bright young men, all, it so happened, with the faces of somewhat foiled Bedlington terriers. With them he liked, at carefree moments, to play a little Pavlovean game of conditioned response. He would pretend acute anxiety over suddenly finding himself caught without sufficient material to fill his next issue, and would rage up and down loudly lamenting the fact that there seemed to be no fresh young talent around whose work he could take the occasion to rush into the breach. It was, as he often said, one of his more pleasant duties as the editor of an influential review not only to help keep alive the institution of letters but to invigorate it with periodic transfusions of healthy new blood. He would keep this up until the brains of his underlings absolutely swam with visions of all those critiques and monographs and tiny jeweled footnotes, so industriously wrought and yet so untimely banished to the oblivion, the academic graveyard, of the bottom dresser drawer, being magically restored to life and crowned with the coveted accolade of print. It was just such a contingency as this that, if successfully met, could bridge the vast black chasm separating instructordom from assistant professorship, and that could still, if only for a little while, that terrible metallic voice which even in the deepest and seemingly safest of post-doctoral sleeps kept snarling like a raspy old gramophone: "Publish or perish, publish or perish, up or out, publish or perish, up or out, publish or perish, up or out." It was not surprising, therefore, that on these occasions there was nothing, literally nothing, that his young men would not do for Buchanan, no humiliation so base that they would not freely and gladly take it from him. They would stand on their hind legs and positively whine to be kicked, just so that they would have the chance to look up at him with that doggy look of craven forgiveness shining wetly from their eyes. They would fawn over him in the most wretchedly obsequious manner, break each other's arms in their rush to light his cigarettes for him, bring him gifts they could not possibly afford, tell him the juiciest kinds of gossip, the absolute secrecy of which they had often sworn a solemn oath to keep, whisper into his ear the most damaging lies about their closest friends and colleagues, offer him their wives if they had any, give him the shirt off their backs and humbly beg his pardon if it was not his size.

Through it all Buchanan would manage to remain resolutely unimpressed. He would tilt comfortably back in his heavy leather swivel chair, put on the snidest of his faint feline smiles, and just let them drool away into his wastebasket. He had, of course, not the slightest intention of ever printing a word they had written. He had, in fact, never been known to print anything that did not come in direct response to the long, intimately newsy letters which he was always sending off to Allen and Lionel and Yvor and Bunny and Tom and Delmore and Richard and Philip and Cleanth and Red and Hannah and Mary. But if ever he felt in imminent danger of being found out—as he very nearly had been once or twice—and of having one of his little pets go mad and fly at his throat, he would toss them from time to time a meaty bone from some old reputation which he had successfully reduced to carcass, and let them fall upon that and crunch it savagely between their long, sharp, angry teeth. That, as a rule, kept them quiet, for if there was one thing they liked to worry and gnaw on, emitting as they did so little ferocious growls of canine delight, it was a reputation, old or new, tough or tender. They hated reputation almost more than they hated one another, not only because it was something which they themselves were secretly dying to get, but because—in the Cranton intellectual world at least—it was intimately related to literature, and literature they hated most of all. They enjoyed their work with Buchanan, and kept at it in spite of his unspeakable treatment of them, because it made them feel superior to literature, and they could participate vicariously in his systematic destruction of it. So long as they were affiliated with the review, they had nothing to do with literature except to peep at it voyeuristically while Buchanan made it writhe and scream on the rack of his own monstrous contempt. Of course they did not produce it themselves and would not have been able to even if Buchanan had let them. But they did produce criticism the way other men might have beheaded dolls or stuck pins in effigies—with a viciousness almost ceremonial under the cold glare of the study lamp in the black of night. Criticism was their method of wreaking vengeance upon literature for being the one thing they could not succeed in by taking a degree or playing politics, and their resentment of it was boundless. But if Buchanan had ever admitted them to the torture chamber by deigning to print any of their efforts, it would quickly have become obvious that in the field of close explicatory sadism they were absolutely without peers, and Buchanan, whose very life depended on being himself absolutely without peers, was far too clever to take a chance on letting a thing like that become obvious.

Waithe had frequently been struck in this connection by a curious fact. At the Saturday-night parties where the young men habitually gathered, mostly, it seemed, to pool the resources of their collective discontent, he had noticed that it was seldom they themselves who revealed their hostility to literature. They, as a rule, did nothing except stand in resentful silence and stare bitterly into their highball glasses or goad one another into long, rather obscurely personal arguments over the quality of the contents of the latest issue of *PMLA*. It appeared to be always in their wives that the hostility came out. The wives were precise incarnations of the ancient Greek ideal, the identical-twin souls of their husbands, but they were souls turned inside out, with all the secret resentments and little itchy places in the family hair shirt exposed for the world to see. What the husbands complained about in the privacy of the bedroom and were much too politically astute to dream of mentioning anywhere else, the wives bore with jut-jawed, hard-heeled indignation straight into their friends' cocktail parties and dumped triumphantly at the feet of the authorities responsible. They had in this respect the indiscriminate generosity of conscienceless cats, and presidents, deans, and department heads had all, from time to time, been obliged over martinis to take delivery of particularly malodorous academic mice. But it was most often visiting literary men who were singled out for such treatment, although in their case the treatment was apt to be far more artful and insidious. If word got around at a party that a writer, especially a writer of reputation, was present, the claws of every young English instructor's wife in the room would come almost audibly unsheathed with a sound very much like the deadly whicker made by the released arrows of King Harry Olivier's gallant longbowmen at the start of the Battle of Agincourt, and a pack of fierce-eyed, grim-lipped Vassar and Smith graduates would converge on their victim, their sinewy bosoms swelling with blood lust. "So *you* are the well-known author we have been hearing so much about," one of them would announce in a voice that might have seen service on the drill fields of Quantico. "My husband and I have just finished reading your new book." On the face of it, there was nothing particularly threatening about this statement. Indeed, it had about it, in spite of the voice, a quality almost of flirtatiousness, intensified perhaps by the fact that, as she made it, the young woman would as a rule stare raptly at the writer's mouth, as if it called up in her emotions which in other circumstances she would have found extremely difficult to control. The writer, thus thrown off his guard, would prepare to say something which he imagined to be disarmingly modest in reply, when he would be vigorously set upon by the others, all, it seemed, with eager opinions about the work in question. Each, it would turn out, had read it in the company of her husband. Each, it would further turn out, had disagreed violently with her husband about its merits and defects. In spite of what her husband had thought, one of them would say, she herself had found it a very good book indeed. Another had personally seen no trace whatever of any influence of William Faulkner, but then what could you expect from a man who had done his whole master's thesis just on the number of times the word "corncob" appears in *Sanctuary*? What if Lionel Trilling *hadn't* especially liked the book, still another would say. Orville Prescott certainly had, and had even devoted an entire column to it. Furthermore, as far as she was concerned, that whole business was sheer nonsense about everything after *The Cold Coming*—which was the title of the writer's first novel—being "an unbroken record of rapidly accelerating spiritual decline." She, for her own part, had never liked *that* book at all.

Normally at some point in the course of this exchange it would come over the writer that in some terribly obscure fashion he was in the process of having his genital heft taken and found wanting. It was never anything very definite, nothing he would in the least have been able to name. Somehow it simply hung in the air of all that eager attentiveness, rather absurdly reminding him of the school nurse that time when, as a little boy, he had been hit in the groin by a baseball. It was not that there was anything overtly malicious about the performance. No one would ever say anything downright insulting; in fact, quite the contrary. Still, an odd, mysterious something would be left behind, some grain of sand in the ego's vaseline, that gave a certain, not quite localized impression of vague discomfort. Then, perhaps hours later, when the writer had finally been abandoned to his drink and the yawning universe, it would occur to him with a crash like that of an empire falling that his heft had not merely been

64

taken but positively made off with. He could even imagine it
dried and shrunken and stuck on top of a pole and being
danced around by a tribe of howling female savages in the
full of the moon. Somehow, while he had been standing there
basking in the glow of all that counterfeit adulation, his
sexual pockets had been picked; little razory scissors had
stealthily clipped away at his manhood, his dignity, his belief
in himself as a writer, until finally he had been left with
nothing but a neat hole in the trousers seat of his integrity.
He had, it seemed, in his fatuous preoccupation, just missed
some unmentioned, perhaps even unmentionable, last chance
of a lifetime; some special excursion train to golden opportunity had pulled out of the station ahead of schedule, leaving him standing on the platform with all his luggage on
board. It was as if his potency had deserted him at the most
embarrassing moment in the dark wedding night of his soul,
and he had unwittingly been made to stand trial for the in-
adequacy of a whole college English association of young
husbands, all of whom had been reading his books in the
company of their wives when they should have been taking
their wives to bed.

There was always something accusingly sexual about these
encounters, some faint but distinctly bitter hint that the
gauntlet of female frustration was being flung down at the
feet of the world's masculinity. Every creative man had sooner
or later, consciously or unconsciously, to stand up and fight
while the wives defended the dishonor of their husbands'
impotence and endeavored to see that the defect became uni-
versal. Only one man was exempt from the challenge, and
that was Buchanan. No gauntlets were ever flung, or dead
mice dropped, at his feet, although any of the wives would, if

they had dared, have eagerly prostrated themselves before him. It was not so much that he held very nearly the power of professional life and death over their husbands. It was more that, because he held this power, the wives came inevitably to associate it with the power of an omnipotent maledom: what could destroy their husbands professionally would no doubt be able to dominate them sexually. As Buchanan bullied their husbands down to lower and lower depths of humiliation, he elevated himself to greater and greater heights of transcendent virility, until at last he completely took over in the minds of the wives the positions which he had forced the husbands to abdicate, replacing their insignificance with an image of himself as magnificent. Ultimately, he became to the wives a sort of heavenly husband-substitute, a mystical abstraction of almost divine proportions, so idealized that the thought of actually having sex with him would have seemed as unreal to them as the thought of going to bed with the Holy Ghost. Still, the potential was always there, the tantalizing possibility that Buchanan might one day shrug off his celestial vestments and descend naked to earth and leadeth them in the path of concupiscence. But it was a possibility that existed only in their own minds, a recurrent erotic daydream with which they gave themselves intellectual orgasms. Buchanan for his part had no intention of letting any such thing happen. However necessary he might be to them, he was to himself a luxury which he could not afford to part with, least of all to them, at any price. Besides, he had long since attained his final silence, his ultimate state of self-induced beatitude. He was alone in the void, secure within the magic circle of his contempt, above history and time and sex and the petty frustrations of man- and womankind, imperturbably wielding power over his little universe like a god he had created out of the graven image of his vast conceit.

4.

That, at any rate, was how Waithe saw Buchanan then, or, more precisely, how he saw, or imagined he saw, other people see him. No one, of course, ever saw Buchanan exactly as he was, and no one, so far as Waithe was concerned, would ever have been likely to. It always in the end came down to a matter of which Buchanan, out of the multitude of observable Buchanans, one was finally content to settle for, and that depended on which Buchanan the man himself decided to let one see. The idea was scarcely conceivable that there was anything more to be seen, that beneath all the masks and disguises there remained some further level still to be penetrated, some ultimate bedrock Buchanan at the center of which one might find entombed like pterodactyl bones the fossilized secret of his real identity. That implied the existence of someone acute enough to do the penetrating, some fantastically ideal psychic archaeologist endowed with an almost saintly capacity not to be taken in and fall prostrate and gaping under the spell of the man's enigmatic charm, the sort of quintessential perfect witness of whom, in the case of Cranton, Waithe had had only the vaguest conception and had finally been obliged out of his own head to invent a fictional surrogate. It also implied, indeed insisted upon, the co-operation of Buchanan himself. It took for granted the gross improbability that he would permit the intrusion by deigning at last to drop his guard, capitulate from his inhuman roles, strike a bargain with the most honest of his several selves, and consent to enter the crowded subway of history and take a seat beside ordinary mortals. But Buchanan struck no bargains, took no seats, had no history. Regardless of the speculations that swarmed around his head like baffled bees around a plundered hive, he seemed to Waithe exactly as he had always seemed: a being out of time and out of history, imprisoned in an eternal present by the unending variety of the roles he played, the perennial hero-villain with a thousand faces, any or none of which might have been his own.

Then suddenly and a little miraculously, quite as if he had all at once inherited a legacy from a relative he did not even know he had, Waithe came into a sort of past for Buchanan. It happened as a result of one of those peculiar collisions of cold fact and remote contingency by which nature, for no apparent reason at all, sometimes imitates bad art, and Waithe was so struck by its dubious character that he was almost tempted to give himself up to it on the theory that anything so horribly trite must contain its particle of truth. The revelation came of course not from Buchanan himself, but from another, a thoroughly implausible other, who had, it seemed, once shared, or at least insinuated himself into, a past with Buchanan and was all eagerness to have it accepted as *the* past, the darkly mysterious, absolutely genuine-article past which Buchanan seemed never to have had, and indeed may never *have* had. For everything in such cases depended upon the quality of the testimony, the unimpeachable word of the witness, and on that score there was in this case somewhat more than reasonable doubt.

The person in question was a very long way from being an ideal witness. There was, in fact, a certain amount of evidence for supposing him capable of perjuring himself if he saw a chance of making over the truth to fit his own rather too neatly prefabricated view of reality. Even if he had been required to swear an oath, it would not necessarily have meant anything, for he was the kind who had been brought up to think of the Bible as literature rather than as Holy Writ, and had from an early age personally preferred *Alice in Wonderland*. He was simply a very young man, a very simple young man, and like Waithe and practically everyone else, he had obviously succumbed long ago to the spell of Buchanan's charm. His imagination—such as it was—had been engaged, then positively caught up and deflowered, by the enigma of the man. All his impressions had become swollen and a little proudly hard, and he had finally been impelled to create out of these impressions and lay at the doorstep of the world his own infant version of a Buchanan past. But his impressions were not in the least to be trusted, for he belonged to that new undergraduate race of cultural *arrivistes* to whom all knowledge is reducible to a two-semester course in the Hundred Great Books, and the life ambition of every studious sophomore is to become one day his own Syntopicon. In an earlier and humbler age he would have been an assiduous clipper of order blanks from the back pages of pulp westerns, a regular subscriber to pamphlets entitled "How to Increase Your Brain Power" and "29 Simple Steps to Mental Mastery," the proud possessor of Dr. Eliot's complete *Five-Foot Shelf*. But so far as Waithe was concerned, he was just another of the many who thought they had seen Buchanan plain, but who had actually only caught a glimpse of him in one of his several roles. In this case, however, even that was unlikely, for the role which seemed to have been glimpsed was one that Waithe could not begin to imagine Buchanan playing. It was in fact a cliché, attributed to the one man among men to whom no cliché could ever have applied, from whom all clichés dropped away like rubber daggers hurled at the armored breast of Zeus. It was Buchanan preposterously seen in the role not simply of a man with a past, but of a man in a state of holy innocence such as had not prevailed on earth since before the fall from Paradise. To the credulous, renovating eye of Shelby (for that was the young man's name), Buchanan had, like Cranton, at one time enjoyed a pristine Edenic condition. The swamps, it seemed, had also in his case once been alive with fish.

The task of meeting the terms which Shelby had, in his bumbling, puppyish way, laid down for the telling of his story ended by costing Waithe a very great deal in patience and nervous energy. It cost him so much, in fact, that after he got his purchase home and unwrapped and set up on the mantelpiece with other curios from the First Buchanan Dynasty, he had good cause to wonder whether he had not been rather drastically outbargained. To get the story he had been obliged to undergo an initiatory test as arduous as Gawain's at the Chapel Perilous, but at the end of it, he could not be sure that he had at all understood what he had gone to so much trouble to learn. The secret of Shelby's Grail—if such there had ever been—remained obscure and mist-shrouded, a thing of romance and legendry, with perhaps one tiny grain of truth buried somewhere deep down in the shifting sands of illusion. So far as Waithe could determine, no desolated kingdom— least of all Buchanan's—had been restored to fertility or even brought to light by his efforts, although Shelby had conclusively proven the fertility of his own powers of invention. He was in this respect rather remarkably like Buchanan himself,

a repressed Southern sentimentalist with a great talent for the
tall tale. But where Buchanan seemed to take on the reality
of everything he imagined, until finally one almost supposed
he had imagined himself, Shelby seemed to think that everything he imagined took on reality. He had the true Southern
rhetorical imagination of disaster, Jamesean in its power to
evoke the subtle sense of the ominous in ordinary things, but
straight rotgut hillbillyean in its joyous indifference to all
civilized laws of accuracy. Whatever he said managed to come
out dripping with Gothic portentousness, thick with sorghumy
insinuations of an indefinable and unutterable something
more than meets the eye, positively reeking of colored-mammy
moonshine spread all over a bedtime-story landscape of
rattling chains, marauding ghosts, and weeping gravestones.
He spoke with the slow, obsessed, hypnotic drawl of an old-
fashioned revival-tent preacher, and at one time he might
have been a tolerably good drummer of ladies' superfine imported, 100 per cent, pure-silk hosiery. Certainly, he had
charm enough, along with a marvelous capacity for believing
everything he said, once he heard what it was, and he probably
would have made the wearing of hosiery sound to the farm
women of north Georgia as sinisterly crucial as the outcome
of the battle of Armageddon. But he had been born out of
his time, and so had no choice but to submit to the conditions
imposed by the fact. He had come North to be educated on
his father's money, had discovered knowledge the way other
young men discover liquor and sex, and had been quickly
and fatally corrupted. Knowledge attracted him like a tantalizing wickedness of the flesh. It appealed to that part of his
imagination which reduced all things to nostrums and witches'
brews, magic signs and lucky pieces; it was the alchemy by

which he might, if he learned enough, be able to transmute everything he fancied into the pure gold of hard fact, be able to make over reality as he wished and still have it turn out to be scientifically true. He looked upon it the way a jaded *vers librist* might look upon the classical form of the sonnet: its strictness was just the therapy his imagination needed. But since he had never got over the technological wonders of the North, he developed the fixed idea that knowledge, like everything else up there, came in packages or could be bought in supermarkets in vitamin-capsule form and taken at ten, two, and four like *Dr. Pepper* down home. He had never really known efficiency before; the concept of mass production was foreign to both his experience and his nature; and so he succumbed to it with the childlike awe and stupendous excess of belief of a savage presented for the first time with a safety match. He expected it to do everything, including light up the world.

5.

Shelby was first introduced to Waithe by a cynical colleague as a kind of circus side-show exhibit, as one of those rare but perfectly genuine two-headed calves that occasionally turned up in the common herd of student bodies to diversify the chores of the academic profession. But it began to come over Waithe on that first encounter that beneath his harmless-looking, even slightly idiotic exterior, Shelby was a natural-born picker of other people's brains, the very worst breed of mental kleptomaniac, the flattering kind, who pretended to sit reverently at one's feet, while he covertly pocketed one's best pearls of wisdom. It even occurred to Waithe that it was he himself, rather than Shelby, who was on exhibit and being peered into and gaped at, while he floated, pickled and helpless, in a big tank of formaldehyde. For Shelby gave the impression of never having seen a real live professor before, at least not in captivity, and kept eying Waithe hopefully as if he expected him at any moment to start reciting the *Encyclopaedia Britannica*. But Waithe would not allow himself to be taken in. He had the almost certain sense that this was all part of an act designed to trick him into revealing some sort of special information, inconsequential to himself, but vital to Shelby. There was something positively Mata-Hari-ish about the boy's superficially innocent desire to know, something cold and calculating and diabolically undercover, as if knowledge were a secret formula he had been commissioned by his government to get at any price. It was clearly not, in Shelby's terms, something to be gained by slow absorption or a leisurely, four-year stroll through the groves of academe. There was too much of an air or urgency about him, too much of a sense of drastic measures needing to be taken right then and there. It was obvious he thought he could get it all at once, perhaps by paying someone a certain sum of money or buying a Do-It-Yourself kit, the way he had come to imagine such things were accomplished up North. From his manner of talking it even seemed possible to suppose that he had given thought to the idea of simply hiring a professor to fly down to his father's plantation for the summer and set up a Platonic symposium for one, with him reading a prescribed set of great books and the professor explaining what the books *meant*, a nice little rustic example of real old-fashioned, man-to-man schooling, a Harvard-educated Mark Hopkins at one end of the log cocktail bar and himself at the other.

He had certainly learned a good deal from someone, and

Waithe had a moment of wondering if perhaps a few of his colleagues had already made the trip. But the more he saw of Shelby, the more it seemed that only Shelby's imagination and not his intelligence had been enlightened, or, more correctly, that a certain *ersatz* enlightenment had gradually been made the clumsy tool of his imagination. It was still the same free-soaring, undisciplined imagination he had always had, but his original hope of directing its flight with the golden wings of scientific accuracy appeared at some point to have been lost; the wings had suddenly turned to wax, had begun to melt in the white heat of truth; and Shelby had been forced to crash-land in the murky sea of half-truth. The lure of what he saw as Northern efficiency had finally proved too much for him, and in his impatience to take full advantage of it, he had settled in the end for a very shoddy imitation of the genuine article. But luckily he never seemed to know the difference. Clichés sprang from his lips with the sure spontaneity of Delphic revelations. He became as heavily eloquent in the clinical vocabulary of his time and generation as he had formerly been in Southern rhetoric, and could hold forth for hours in all the insufficiently unknown tongues of psychiatry, sociology, anthropology, and *Life* magazine editorials. He was especially persuasive on the subjects of "silence" and "conformity"—the double crosses on which so many of the would-be Christs of his age group had been Luce-ified—and he had picked up the cocktail-party manner of speaking with that fashionably dead objectivity of one long accustomed to seeing himself as a mere statistic, a dot on a probability curve, a figure of risk on an insurance-company actuarial table, a radioactive mote in the dust of an atomic explosion. He saw everything in terms of graphs, norms, surveys, case histories, and imminent catastrophes: all the mechanisms that were meant to stand for, evaluate, compute, measure, explain, and do away with the reality which his imagination sought to verify and control through one quick application of hard fact.

Even in the realm of human affairs he appeared to think he had found the formula, the rule, the one sublime and perfect equation. Sex had overtaken him rather late in life and had scarcely had time to become personal before knowledge and the reading of certain books had objectified it into simply another source of information, another way of explaining to himself and the world just how things were. Every unhappy female of his acquaintance was obviously in love with her father; every unhappy male was a clear case of repressed homosexuality; every man, woman, and child of whatever degree of unhappiness seemed to him a tangled, overgrown jungle of thwarted libidinous cravings, sibling rivalries, ego malfunctions. In a similar way he had fallen under the spell of literary criticism and, ironically enough, had been particularly stricken by the works of the recent Southern school, a few of whose members he vaguely recalled having as a small child actually been kissed by, but whom until very recently he had always thought of as poets. He had even once learned by heart the whole of the "Ode to the Confederate Dead" and remembered having, on the occasion of his ninth or tenth birthday, recited it with intonations of great feeling before an assemblage of his father's weekend guests, of whom the author himself was one. But he had long since forgotten every line of the poem, had, as it were, kept pace with the poets in their migration northward from the obscure outposts of poetic fancy into the cleared and more civilized territories of critical reason. As a result, he had found their formulations peculiarly

75

congenial to his newly acquired Northern state of mind, if only because they were formulations *of* that state of mind acquired in exactly the same way he had acquired it—through being rather precipitately transplanted from one order of reality to another of quite a different kind. He therefore had no trouble at all in attributing every failure of courtesy, dignity, or moral courage which he witnessed in the North to the truth of one or more of these formulations—to the extreme dissociation of sensibility in the modern world (meaning, of course, the North), the terrible division of the modern age (meaning, of course, the division of the country into two sections following the War between the States), the loss of contact with a traditional society (meaning, of course, the sort of society alleged to have flourished in the ante-bellum South), the disastrous split between head and heart knowledge (meaning, of course, the split of which Shelby himself, since leaving the South, had become a more and more glaring example). It was all somehow part of a common lost heritage, a familiar vocabulary and rhetoric, revised and adapted to the conditions of the exile which it served to explain. It did not matter in the slightest that, by the time it got to Shelby, it had become a cliché. It was the one cliché among all the clichés he had acquired that seemed to have real point, that spoke to him with real directness and force, that seemed to bring him into the closest touch with the reality he sought to understand. The fact that it ended by separating him completely from that reality, from all reality, was a truth to which he was conveniently and totally oblivious. The only thing that mattered was that it *felt* true; it appealed to his imagination; it structured the tumult of his mind. If it also made him into something of a monster, his friends were ready to take the responsibility for that. After all, they were natives of the North, and it was obviously the North that had changed him into what he had become.

In view of all this, it was not surprising that the image of Buchanan which had become fixed in Shelby's mind—particularly since he had acquired the informed perspective of a Northern *déraciné*—was the image of a man divorced from his Edenic origins, in exile from his natural community, and perverted by his thwarted creative drives into a power-mad literary Napoleon. It was, in fact, an altogether proper, predictable, and, as it then seemed to Waithe, even necessary image for Shelby to have created, since it nicely combined the most melodramatic features of his inborn Southern imagination with the hoariest stereotypes of his new-found Northern enlightenment. It was also—and this Waithe took just pride in having discerned—a partial portrait of Shelby himself, done by his own hand before his own mirror, but craftily passed off, in the devious fashion of the unconscious mind, as an exact likeness of Buchanan. It was quite simply the work of the hidden monitor in Shelby, surveying with the glittering cold eye of truth his doubtful dealings in the pseudo-intellectual world and condemning him for being himself a refugee from his natural time and place, an outcast from his own Eden, a traitor to the cause of his own spiritual identity and completeness. It even occurred to Waithe that the whole of Shelby's infatuation with knowledge, with the language and values of alienation, whether in the social sciences or Southern criticism, might also have been the work of this little puritanical district attorney busily preparing his case against the mentally delinquent Shelby. Certainly, there was abundant evidence for supposing that the Buchanan whose story

Shelby finally told to Waithe was a Buchanan whom Shelby had unwittingly created in his own image, was no more, in fact, than Buchanan seen in another of his roles, but a role forced upon him this time by a person who needed him to play that particular role, so that through it he might dramatize and discharge his own unconscious sense of guilt.

Waithe was nonetheless, in spite of his several reservations, stuck with Shelby's story. It was quite simply all there was to go on in the way of a past for Buchanan, the one ray of light, however flickering and dim, that he had to turn on the dark history of the man toward whom he, no less than Shelby, had strongly equivocal feelings—feelings that pressed him like insistent plaintiffs for some kind of action, no matter how tentative, against the day when he would himself be obliged to act as district attorney and prosecute the case before the bar of his own conscience. Shelby was so far the only shred of tangible evidence he had, was the one unquestionably material witness who had been on the scene, and even if his word could not always be trusted, even if there were grounds for supposing him in league with the mysterious prisoner in the dock, Waithe had no choice but to hear his testimony, and then do his own revising, make his own allowances, and perhaps arrive that way at at least a rough approximation of a truth. There was no such thing as *the* truth, not, at any rate, where Buchanan was concerned. Waithe had long ago given up that idea, for there had, at one time or another, been too many witnesses—he himself by no means the least of them—who had all had their own stories and their own reasons for having the particular stories they had. All of them seemed sooner or later to have entered into a sort of private conspiracy with Buchanan, to have fallen into debt to him, or bought stock in his company. All of them eventually saw him in terms of their vested interests in him, and what they saw, therefore, became a fabrication, an invention, or, at the very most, a compromise between what they had to be loyal to in their own secret hearts—for the sake, perhaps, of their own secret bank accounts—and those aspects of his nature which their hearts and their bank accounts would permit them to see. Shelby, in this sense, was simply another investor, although one of the very first, and while Waithe had reason to suspect it was large, the actual size of his holdings in Buchanan stock was shrouded in that discreet mystery by which civilization protects its financial as well as its moral commitments.

His story was both a product of not wholly disinterested vision and a confession, a deeply subterranean working out in the form of biased biography of a personal problem. It did not come to Waithe all at once, but over the months that he knew Shelby, it came to him in pieces—as, indeed, parts and hints of it, through rumors and the oblique allegations of gossip, had already come to him from other sources—and the coherence it finally came to have derived not from any essential structure within it, but from the structure which Shelby laboriously imposed upon it out of his own need for coherence, and which Waithe then imposed upon Shelby's out of his. As Shelby talked on scattered evenings in his slow, hesitant, at times irritatingly fumbling way—for on the subject of Buchanan his normal eloquence seemed strangely to desert him—Waithe found himself being drawn more and more into the narrative, making the story more and more completely his own, until at last he ended by telling it to himself in his own words. He could not then have said how much of it he consciously understood, or even how much there was in it to understand. He knew only that for some reason it impressed him. As Shelby himself might have said, it *felt* right. It squared somehow with his deeply psychic sense of the real. In a peculiar way, it was the story out of all the possible stories of Buchanan's past which he himself would finally have settled upon, if he had been obliged to create one out of what he knew of the man. It quite simply *fit*, perhaps because of its very patness, its very triteness, the very openness of its acceptance of the obvious in life. But that, oddly enough, was the principal thing which in the end made Waithe suspicious of it and caused him to handle it gingerly as if it were the purest dynamite, for somewhere deep down inside him, deeper even than his sense of the real, at a point, in fact, where that sense could easily have been undermined, it seemed to represent a threat to his integrity, to his own almost frantically necessary belief in the recurring originality of life.

CHAPTER IV

1.

THE CHARACTERIZING NOTE OF SHELBY'S NAR-
rative—the note, at least, which seemed, as he thought back
upon it, to characterize it most forcibly for Waithe—was the
note, high-pitched and loud, of a woman's voice raised in anger
out of the cool, almost Sabbatical quiet of a summer afternoon. It was a voice overheard, quite unintentionally eaves-
dropped on, by the boy Shelby and, therefore, retained by him
in imaginative escrow with those other items stumbled upon
or stolen from the emotional treasury of adulthood, until the
day came when chance, like the inexplicable breaking of a
rusty lock, would discover them all yellowed and old and release them again upon the market of the world's fatality. That
day for Shelby had rather recently come and gone; chance had
broken in upon him in the form of the unexpected discovery
of Buchanan, older if not yellowed, living in Cranton; and
with that discovery the sound of the voice had returned to him
with Proustian suddenness, but returned now in the full context of its significance, against the ratifying background of its
achieved history. It rose now on the superheated air of his
imagination, as it had once risen on the cool air of that far-off
summer afternoon, like some mad harpy's voice screeching its

curse down all the guilt-concealing corridors of time, upon all the living and the dead. Only now as he thought, knowing what he now knew, remembering himself standing there in the doorway of his father's house, uncertain whether to run or die, it seemed to him the voice of all womankind crying out in righteous idealism against the weak, betraying factualness of men. That, at any rate, was how he said it seemed, how he had romanticized it into seeming, how his obsessed, disaster-haunted imagination had convinced him it had seemed. Actually, however, what the voice had said on that occasion was nothing very startling or remarkable, or at least it did not seem so to Waithe. There had not really been very much of an outburst for the boy Shelby to overhear; no very astounding revelation had been exploded upon the gentle quiet of that decorous afternoon. Such explosion as there had been had obviously occurred mostly in Shelby's own head. But it had nonetheless just as obviously meant a great deal to him. It had held at the time, and apparently still held for him, a vast quantity of somber significance of a kind that exceeded all the known facts of the case, and yet could not exceed the capacity of his imagination to cast over the facts a sinister gray light of prescience. It seemed that even at the moment of first hearing it, the voice had spoken to him in a tone of clearly recognizable warning, not so much through what it said as through its sound, and even though he could not have told then what it warned of, he did know to whom it belonged, and that somehow seemed to him warning enough. It was, after all, the voice of the woman who for twenty years had been Buchanan's wife, and who, although no one had yet been informed of it, planned soon to be his wife no longer. Perhaps the mere fact that it was Buchanan's wife who had spoken was what had impressed

Shelby, or perhaps he had sensed in what she had said the warning that she would soon cease to be. But whichever it was, coming as they did out of the clean silence and calm of that summer afternoon, her words had been heavy with ominous implication for him, and standing there hearing them, he had been quite simply appalled. *Tawk, tawk, tawk,* she had cried in her shrill nasal accent. *Thayt's awl he evah does naow, daym him to Hayl. Is tawk, tawk, tawk.* Simple words, ordinary words, but in them the boy Shelby had caught the faint but unmistakable note of doom. They seemed to resound in his memory through all the years that now separated him from that moment, and to have grown with time into a charged rhetoric of impending catastrophe, as though somewhere out there beyond the shadows on the lawn that summer afternoon an empire had been about to fall, or some cosmic betrayal had been planned to steal away the radiance from the sun.

2.

That had been the beginning, the first hint, at least so far as Shelby knew, of Buchanan's imminent expulsion out of a paradise which he could no longer afford to maintain, which, in fact, seemed no longer *there* to be maintained. But to understand the meaning it had for Shelby one had to go back— as he himself had done in his account of it to Waithe—to the time before the beginning, to the time when the paradise was still intact, and understand the role which Buchanan had then played in Shelby's life. It was evidently Buchanan's Ur-role, the first and best of his career, and perhaps the one that came closest to being a true projection of his original nature. Certainly, there was far less reason for it to have been a *role* than there was for any of the others he had since played; it even seemed to Shelby as he thought back over it that there was no reason at all, since at that time Buchanan could have had nothing whatever to hide. But whether he had or not, the effect of absolute sincerity which he managed to create must have been greatly enhanced by the fact that he was performing before an uncritical audience of one, and of one, furthermore, who, unlike almost all Buchanan's subsequent audiences, had no vested interests in pretending to believe, but who believed simply because he wanted to and had to, in answer to the deeply compelling needs of his own secret heart. There was even a possibility that, for the one time in his life, Buchanan himself had believed, that all his reasons for not believing, like all his reasons for playing his subsequent roles, had resulted from the ultimate collapse of that first role, the loss, that is, of his first innocence. But that, in the developing context of Shelby's narrative, seemed to Waithe purely conjectural and beside the point, a sentimental break in the flow of directly observed events, an effort on Shelby's part to justify to himself, in the light of his present knowledge, what had occurred, to keep sacred, perhaps, the memory of his own first innocence. The truth was that Shelby had at that time, rightly or wrongly, succumbed to Buchanan's spell, and Waithe thought it important that the unvarnished fact be allowed to remain in the record. Buchanan then was quite obviously a kind of god to Shelby, the very greatest thing there was and, as Shelby had apparently since come to feel, the very greatest thing there was ever likely to be in his world. He was rock, fortress, haven of refuge, impregnable outpost of last defense—in short, a one-man spiritual Gibraltar guarding the exposed straits of Shelby's will to believe—but he was also and above all a very real, whole, and vital human being who inevitably became both a substitute for Shelby's father and a living refutation of everything his father was and stood for. Whenever Shelby began in somber moments to entertain the idea that all men were like his father, he had Buchanan to point to, to bolster his faith with, to argue his case before, as a sort of higher court of emotional appeal. For in his hopefully, even desperately credulous mind, Buchanan and his father stood at opposite poles in the heavily magnetized field of his vision of life. But even though he was drawn irresistibly to the one, he sensed that the other was somehow essential to preserve the tension from which his attraction drew its fatal force.

3.

Just what Shelby's father had been like at that time was another matter for conjecture. The exact information seemed to be locked away somewhere in the remote recesses of Shelby's unconscious mind, and Waithe had been obliged to piece together such impression as he had out of odd bits and scraps of remarks dropped here and there in the course of Shelby's narrative. But evidently the boy had had only the most superficial relationship with his father—which, as is usual in such cases, really meant that he had had no relationship at all—and almost from the beginning even of that relationship, the father's image had suffered by comparison with the image of Buchanan which Shelby had rather triumphantly held up against it. Waithe inferred, however, that he had appeared then, and seemed still to appear to Shelby, to be a man peculiarly lacking in those qualities of inward definition by which the majority of men identify themselves as human beings and take their place as individual entities in the society of other men. Everything about him, everything that related him in any way at all to his surroundings—and that relationship, too, was tenuous—seemed to have been inherited from the past or somehow handed down to him like outgrown clothing by a welfare organization of charitable ancestors. He seemed never in his lifetime to have initiated a single action in his own behalf, to have bought a single item strictly for his personal use. He was a living repository of other people's long-ago choices in the apparel and furniture of being, a walking rag bag and antique shop of curiosities discarded along the route of history. The past was always at and on his back, and he wore it and lived with it with the ill-fitting dignity of one totally oblivious of the fact that he could have afforded the amenities of a made-to-measure world. His moral center—if such he had ever had—had presumably been shot away in the Civil War. At least the castration of his line—and he, of course, would be the last of it—appeared to date from that historic event. But even that had happened to him vicariously and by inheritance; a hand-me-down eunuchhood had been purchased for him from a humble hill-farmer, himself already bankrupt, who had been paid to take his paternal grandfather's place in battle. This same grandfather had, with comparable thoughtfulness, bequeathed him his plantation—which had also, upon the payment of a much larger sum of money, miraculously escaped the war—and with it the manners, privileges, and graces proper to the station to which the ownership of a plantation naturally elevated him. In all the years of his tenancy the elder Shelby had apparently never once felt the need to question, depart from, or modify in the slightest degree the terms of the trust which his ancestor had so generously and with such acute vision placed in him. He had, in fact, abided by them through all those years with the supreme serenity of a man for whom time had, at some convenient moment well before his birth, quite simply stopped, and nothing whatever had happened in the world since then, including in particular the odd proceedings at Appomattox. He went about fulfilling his obligations to the past as though, in view of his patrimony, the past had an absolute claim on him, as though a hundred-year mortgage had been taken out on his soul, and he was bound by ties of indebtedness running back through a war that for him had never even begun, let alone ended, to a creditor who had never died and a contract on which the ink of the signature was as fresh as yesterday. It was not surprising, therefore, that he had, properly speaking, no contemporary existence of any kind, that everything he did belonged to the ritual of a tradition that lived on in him as simply and naturally, as indisputably *present*, as his beating heart. On every morning of his life except the Sabbath he rode around his property on a fine milk-white stallion that was exactly like, because a multi-filial offspring of, the one his grandfather used to ride. Arriving at the little settlement of shanties that housed his Negro workmen, themselves the descendants of his grandfather's Negro slaves, he would pause and exchange a courteous word with their womenfolk, remembering always to inquire after the health and welfare of the children, all of whom he took gentle pride in being able to call by name. Then he would ride on and make his rounds, stopping at last on a certain grassy slope from which, each morning at precisely nine o'clock, it was his custom—as it had been his grandfather's—to survey at leisure his broad green acres and speculate on the size and quality of the approaching harvest. Seated there, very erect in the saddle, his classic face immobilized in thought, he bore a striking resemblance to the statue of General Lee in Richmond, but a Lee untested and unmarked by the fateful challenges of either war or history, a Lee, in fact, through whose ordered, tranquil mind the thought of surrender had simply never had cause to pass.

It was this image of his father—done, as it were, in bronze—that remained with Shelby the longest of any of the early memories he had of him: the image of a man who, like the carcass of some prehistoric specimen out of a lost continent of science fiction, had miraculously been preserved intact into the present day, and had been stuffed and put on display in a public museum of unnatural history. He was perhaps the sole surviving proof of what the ante-bellum South had been really like, what had really been behind the romantic façade which legend had raised upon the fatuous scaffolding of that time, and which the modern Southern poets had sentimentalized into a sort of Arcadian backdrop for their own lost cultural Eden. But although Shelby could not have been consciously aware of it then, it might well have been his father's obscure sense of his indebtedness to that legend, of the necessity that it survive so that he could survive, that first led him to admire —without, of course, in the least understanding—the work of those poets, and to find reassurance in their presence as regular guests in his home. It might have been that very fatuousness, deliberately courted in the form of his father's hospitality, that had ended by introducing Buchanan into Shelby's life, and giving the boy his first chance to measure the real against the unreal, the living against the dead. For over the years Buchanan became the most frequent and favored of his father's guests; a peculiar friendship developed between the two men; and finally one autumn morning very early, while Shelby was still asleep, Buchanan arrived with his wife, books, and baggage to stay, it seemed, for good. The father had had fixed over for him a little house out on the edge of the estate, a house secluded enough for the writing of poetry and already sanctified for the labors of the spirit by Shelby's great-grand-father, who had been known to retreat there on long-ago Sunday afternoons to play his violin and meditate upon the finer questions of infinity.

4.

So began for Shelby a relationship that continued through the most impressionable time of his youth and that he always remembered as having been conducted in an atmosphere of, at least to him, almost dreamlike happiness. To say that he was enchanted was to say only what Waithe had long since inferred from the whole complexion of his view of that part of his past with Buchanan. He was hypnotized, enthralled, wholly and delightfully captivated. Buchanan caught at his awakening imagination and charged it with a sense of infinite promise and expectation such as he had never known, or could have expected to know, in the shuttered and antique-crowded confines of his father's world. Buchanan was quite simply the first glimpse he had ever had of the future as an entity separate and distinct from the past, of time not as a dark corridor running back to the communal grave of tradition, but as a sun-filled doorway opening onto a clear and limitless prospect of exciting things to come.

Yet even as he recalled how vividly he had once had these feelings, Shelby was somewhat at a loss to account for their origins. They had come upon him at an age when he had been equipped only to experience, not to understand them, so that they lay now at the edges of his mind divorced forever from the precise circumstances which had aroused them, explicable solely as they related to the cluster of vague images he had managed to salvage from his memory of certain moments he had shared at the time with Buchanan. But even at that, his high talent for melodrama, for raising everything to the tenth power of emotionality, had obviously worked in secret upon those moments and so charged them with significance that Waithe felt certain they far exceeded in splendor any that mere life could produce, and, for that matter, any evidence that Shelby could produce for thinking them splendid. Yet he clearly thought them so; he insisted they had been so; and Waithe had no recourse but to make the best of that insistence, even as he struggled like a poor swimmer to keep his own head above water and his feet in some kind of frequent touch with solid bottom. For Shelby with all his insistence, perhaps even exactly because of the thing in him which made him insist, was a man who had had a definite impression of Buchanan at a crucial moment in his life, and it was that impression, whether soundly based on fact or freely elaborated out of an uncertain combination of fact and fancy, that Waithe wanted most to have. He therefore left the exact manner of its conveyance to Shelby's discretion, knowing that even his lapses from discretion would be important, not only for what they revealed about the depth of his own involvement, but for the light they might shed on the mystery of how a man like Buchanan could once have sustained such an involvement, regardless of its depth.

Actually, however, Shelby's account of that involvement— once he had ceased insisting upon its splendor and begun the telling—was neither indiscreet nor freely elaborated. On the contrary, it had about it a kind of fumbling honesty which Waithe could not help but admire, as well as a kind of innocent wonderment, as if Shelby himself were learning as he talked, as if he had never really formulated it to himself before the moment of talking, and had to start with the simplest things, the very barest beginnings. He recalled, for instance, that it was Buchanan who had taught him all he knew—and until then he had not even wanted to know—about nature and wildlife, who had taken him on long walks through the woods and had pointed out and named, in both Latin and English, the various kinds of trees and flowers. It was Buchanan who had sat with him in the evenings out on the porch of the little house and told him about the stars, the constellations, the spiral nebulae, the Milky Way and its probable distance from the earth, Buchanan who later on had introduced him to literature—not as a key or any kind of answer, but as an end, a good, in itself—and had nurtured in him the beginnings of taste. He remembered how on late fall days they had worked together in the crisp air sawing up dead pine trees which they had pushed down and dragged in from the woods, and how Buchanan had bent over the big chopping block as he split the sawn logs, his ax seeming to drop by its own weight down the clean, straight grain of the pine, the two halves of the logs falling apart as easily and neatly as if they had been pasted together. He also remembered how, as he had wandered out to the little house on his almost daily visits, he would sometimes catch a glimpse through the open doorway of Buchanan seated at his desk, his books and papers piled high around him, other papers scattered on the floor at his feet, in deep concentration on something he was writing, his intent face luminous in the sun's rays slanting through the window—the young poet Buchanan with the light of destiny upon him. At such times Shelby would always pause and turn away, sensing obscurely that this was an area of Buchanan's life upon which he must not intrude, in which, even if invited to, he could not allow himself to share, if only for the sake of his own almost mystical belief in its sanctity. At other times, too, when he would come out in the evenings and, stopping on the path, see Buchanan and his wife sitting close together on the front steps in the early dark, he would also turn away, again knowing that the spell of privacy, of personal communion, must be kept inviolate. It was not merely that Shelby was beginning even then to feel the stirrings of discretion. It was, perhaps even more remarkably, that he was beginning to sense the importance of distance in maintaining the system of delicate tensions on which his relationship with Buchanan, as well as his vision of Buchanan, had come to depend. For the shared and the unshared moments, the glimpses of Buchanan as counseling friend and as private person, all came together in Shelby's mind to form an ultimate image which he desperately wanted to keep, and which, even though it was now faded and out-of-date, he apparently still wanted to keep in the locket of his memory of that time—an image of Buchanan as a sort of sacred, omnipotent mentor in the rite of passage which had conducted him out of the sterility of his father's world and brought about his initiation into at least a first awareness of the possibility of a vital life.

But there shortly came a time when the distance between the public and the private sides of Buchanan's nature began of its own accord to diminish, when Shelby, in spite of himself, slowly began to share a little in all that had formerly been unknown and secret, personal and inviolable. As he grew older, he was more and more frequently present on evenings when the poets, who were officially the guests of his father, would manage to steal away with Buchanan after some interminable social affair and come out to the little house to drink and talk. There was always something faintly clandestine about these gatherings, a subtle air of conspiracy and intrigue, which intensified for Shelby the feeling he already had that, just by being there, he was violating a law of his own conscience. It was not merely that they were held without his father's knowledge or approval. If his father had known of them, he would undoubtedly have been perplexed rather than offended, simply unable to understand why they could not just as well have taken place in the more gracious circumstances of his living room. There was no question, however, but that a certain small portion of their forbidden flavor was associated, at least in Shelby's mind, with the fact that his father did *not* know and *might* have been offended. But the more evident fact still was that these evenings at the little house seemed genuinely subversive in their own right, and in a way that involved the father only initially as a sort of catalytic agent or only remotely as a sort of abstract authority against which a pleasant tension could be generated. The poets would huddle around Buchanan's kitchen table like revolutionists plotting an attack on the imperial palace. In their obvious relief at no longer having to be on their best behavior, no longer having to be nice to some fatuous old lady who simply adored poets but who never read poetry, they drank too much too quickly and managed to make everything they said sound heavy with mysterious portent. Their faces in the light of the single candle burning on the table looked flushed and eager and even sinister. They spoke guardedly—as it seemed to Shelby—of "the movement" and of certain individuals as being "one of us" and of strategies and maneuvers as if of troops and battle tactics. Shelby would not have been surprised if at any moment one of them had produced from his pocket a crude map showing the exact location of enemy gun emplacements and barbed-wire barricades. For there seemed to *be* an enemy, a hostile body in power, an anonymous "they" who had all the authority. But it also seemed that the enemy was gravely handicapped by stupidity and would soon be overthrown in one brilliantly executed *coup* by the underground forces of enlightenment.

"The movement," Shelby finally learned, was to be launched not with bombs and assassinations but with poetry, a new kind of poetry militant in its formal strictness, its metaphorical precision, and employing the weapons of irony and wit upon materials drawn from the rich resources of Southern tradition and Southern agrarian life, the vigorous native resources in which their culture abounded and in which the industrial North—where, Shelby gathered, the enemy had its headquarters—was so sadly deficient. The right time for action was apparently still some distance away, but until it arrived, there was a great deal of work to be done. All sorts of plans had to be made and put into secret and effective operation; certain key people in positions of influence had to be won over; certain key publications had to be infiltrated and their editorial policies sabotaged; the appearance of certain subversive articles had to be arranged for; above all, the reputations of certain writers had to be publicly re-examined, and those aspects of their work which seemed, or could be made to seem, favorable to the Southern cause had to be subtly embroidered upon until they became generally accepted as the defining features of the

work. Most of the writers mentioned were already familiar to
Shelby as a result of Buchanan's careful tutelage, but he had
never before had occasion to think of them as potential sources
of revolutionary power. To the poets, however, Eliot, Pound,
Yeats, Hopkins, and Donne seemed to represent a sort of literary Politburo to whose writings all important questions of
form and doctrine had ultimately to be referred. The work of
Eliot they cited in the catechistic manner of old-time Bolshe-
viks invoking the principles of *Das Kapital,* and one might
have judged from the reverence with which they talked of Hopkins and Donne that these writers had co-authored a poetic
equivalent of the *Communist Manifesto.* As a silent witness
to such discussions Shelby often felt like a probational junior
Party member whose loyalties were being secretly tested, and
at other times, when he was unable to share in the prevailing
enthusiasm, like an undercover agent for some conservative
enemy faction. But he gradually came to realize that, whatever
his own feelings may have been, the gatherings were in a very
fundamental way essential to Buchanan. It was obvious that
he depended on them far more than they depended on him.
They seemed to hold him up somehow and sustain him in his
commitment to the solitary role of practicing poet, to recharge
his creative batteries just when they threatened to go dead, to
afford him a reassuring sense of the existence of another and
more meaningful world than the one in which he lived, isolated as he was in the alien territory of Shelby's father's way of
life. They appeared to give his dedication, his belief in himself
and his work, something tangible to hang onto at those moments when he must have felt that he was struggling to function in a vacuum, when he must have wondered whether he
could hold out much longer against the nothingness that en-

closed him on all sides like an uninhabited jungle surrounding some last outpost of cultural progress. Whether he ever actually believed in "the movement," the cause of the new Southern renaissance, was of course uncertain and perhaps in the end beside the point. The important thing was that it was a symbol of promises and potentialities, of a vaguely attainable goal toward which he could point his energies, or simply in whose existence he could find a measure of security and purpose. That, at any rate, was how it seemed to Shelby then, and how it continued to seem through all those crucial years when his contradictory images of Buchanan as kindly mentor and as unapproachable god seemed about to give way at last to a single enduring image of Buchanan as intimate friend.

Or that, more correctly, was how Shelby *said* it seemed, that was *his* view of what had occurred, and it was on the warning note of this realization that Waithe's absorption in the narrative abruptly ceased. He had been aware for some time of a certain sag in his willingness to believe, and now his critical sense reasserted itself in full force and at once shifted the balance of his perspective from that of passive listener to that of judge. For the truth was that Waithe, as he listened, had been finding Shelby's story steadily harder to swallow. Its initial charm—the very charm of its fumbling honesty—had somewhere along the way worn thin, and Waithe had subconsciously begun to realize that Shelby not only *was* fumbling but that his honesty was taking on an unmistakable tone of labor. It was not that he had started to lie. It was more that his honesty seemed, as it fumbled, to find less and less to work with; the thing fumbled *for* seemed to become harder to grasp; and the line between truth and rather desperately contrived fancy grew increasingly indistinct. The evidence, for one thing, which

Shelby offered in support of certain of his feelings about Buchanan was very far from being complete or conclusive. Such facts as there were seemed peculiarly barren and dead, as though in trying to extract their full significance, Shelby had squeezed all the emotional juice out of them. Waithe was reminded once again of how thoroughly Shelby's imagination had worked over the early part of his experience with Buchanan, and of how, as a result, there actually were, properly speaking, no more facts left to be had. There were only the impressions which, in his later thinking on that experience, he had been able to derive from the facts, but which, through being derived, had annihilated the facts and taken their place in his consciousness. He was left now only with the impressions, suspended as it were in the void of his ransacking imagination. He had no real evidence to give for the high quality which he obviously believed his relationship with Buchanan to have possessed, nor was his account of Buchanan's charm and force of character in any way equal to the task of communicating his sense of that charm and force. As for the poets who loomed so large in the narrative, they struck Waithe as having no reality whatever. Certainly, they did not seem like figures which Shelby had drawn from living memory, but rather like fabrications which, in retrospect, he had created out of his maturer idea of how they *must have been*. They sounded, in fact, as though he had dreamed them up out of his extensive readings in American literary history, popular spy thrillers, and the back numbers of *New Masses*. Yet they were clearly meant to serve the purpose of explaining and justifying one of his strongest impressions, which was that Buchanan at that time had been peculiarly centered in a world of creativity, had belonged to a developing poetic movement, and had been living in close conjunction with his imaginative sources. How else could he account for his equally strong impression that something somehow had gone wrong?—for evidently something had. The intimate relationship he had seemed on the verge of having with Buchanan had simply caved in; some psychic barricade deep down inside the man had crumbled away; and the unfortunate fall from the paradise of innocence and artistic dedication had commenced.

5.

Shelby was by no means sure just how or when this had happened, but it seemed to date in his memory from the time he had first heard the sound of the woman's voice raised in anger on that quiet summer afternoon, and had recognized it as the voice of Buchanan's wife. He had, of course, been vaguely aware some time before then that things were not altogether well out at the little house, but until that moment of almost traumatic aural insight he had been unable to localize his scattered impressions of crisis. On his desultory walks to and from visits with Buchanan he had, however, frequently overheard, and tried not to notice, certain sounds of bickering, and had once, without meaning to, listened for a very long time to Buchanan's voice droning on and on up and down the scale of bafflement and rage—*awl he evah does naow . . . is tawk, tawk, tawk*—as if he were conducting some sort of unholy inquisition, with himself acting as both prosecutor and victim. Then there had been the warm spring night when Shelby had come out and seen through the open doorway Buchanan sitting at his desk, as he had so often seen him, but now quite obviously drunk, his head in his hands, a bottle of whiskey beside him, staring blankly down at the scattered papers in front of him, as though he were seeing them now for the first time, as though the writing on them had suddenly been transformed into a language he could not comprehend, or mocking and obscene phrases had been scrawled there by the hand of a stranger. Very evidently something *had* gone wrong, disastrously wrong, and about the nature of that something the maturer, reflective Shelby had evolved over the years several theories with which he had filled in and finally blotted out of his mind altogether the naïve perplexity of his younger self. They were all, so far as they went, tenable enough theories, if one subscribed to certain fashionable notions of history and the causes of human conduct. But they seemed much too fashionable to Waithe, much too easily and hastily arrived at, and much too confidently applied to a man who, in Waithe's opinion, had always been far more than the sum of his parts, far larger than any of the neat psychological cubbyholes into which people tried to fit him. None of Shelby's theories sounded as though they had cost him enough, in either insight or compassion. They sounded, in fact, as though he had bought them wholesale at some intellectual bargain counter of twentieth-century half-truths, the same sort of counter at which he had bought the poets. His theories, however, were better than his poets, if only because he cared much more about them. They were essential somehow—as the poets were not—to the tense order of his mind, to the tidiness of the mental package which he had made of his impressions of Buchanan's past. Above all, they were part of his way of solving for himself a mystery before which his heart had once faltered and come close to breaking, and from which his mind had tried to rescue him by substituting answers, *any* answers, for the unappeasable anguish of forever not knowing.

99

At the bottom of all Shelby's theories, and at the center of his boyhood disillusionment, was the bitter conviction that somewhere along the line Buchanan had simply lost his nerve. As Shelby put it in rough paraphrase of Conrad, Buchanan at some point had no longer found it possible to hold himself up in the destructive element solely by the exertions of his hands and feet. Or, put more precisely, the element in which he found himself immersed had *become* destructive the moment he discovered there was nothing to hold him up *except* his own exertions. The learning swimmer, realizing that he was swimming unaided for the first time, had suddenly been overcome by panic and begun to sink. But there *were* several extenuating circumstances. The movement of which Shelby felt Buchanan had initially been a part had over the years slowly withdrawn its support from him, had ceased to hold him up, not so much because it had failed—although in a sense it had—but because in another sense it had succeeded. It had become recognized as a central development in modern poetry and been assimilated into both the public domain and the institution of literature. It was, in fact, no longer a movement at all but part of the established order, the official hierarchy against which new movements led by new groups of radical young poets were already in revolt. Its original aims had, to be sure, for the most part not been achieved. The dream of a Southern agrarian renaissance was still a dream, or more correctly, it had come to be recognized even by its proponents for what it had been from the beginning—an illusion based on nostalgia for a paradise that could never have existed. But nothing in this world is more generously rewarded than honest repentance for youthful mistakes, particularly when they are mistakes born of idealistic strivings to reform this world, and the proof lay in the fact that most of Buchanan's cohorts had gone over or—as Shelby uncharitably put it—*sold out* to the enemy at considerable profit to themselves in prestige and security. The revolutionary friends had departed North, leaving no addresses except academic ones. In the North among their former foes, they had had conferred upon them the new *ersatz* accolade of literary success—appointments to well-paying jobs in the better universities, where they lectured on the poetry of their former friends. Concurrently with this development, the bottom seemed to have fallen out of the old-style literary life. The function of the independent writer such as Buchanan had been had gradually become irrelevant, an interesting oddity, at best a quaint survival rather like Shelby's father, but with the difference that the father had taken pains to preserve the conditions of his survival, while Buchanan and his kind had shored no fragments against their illusion's ruin. They had gone on as they always had, single-mindedly cultivating the broad acres of their ancestral integrity, and the historical weather had changed; a drought had set in; and the overworked land had dried up and blown away. Where they had once been sustained by the possibility of becoming great men, they now faced a situation in which it seemed taken for granted that all the great men had long since been. The solitary creation of literature had at some point given way to generalized criticism of it; it suddenly seemed more important to have read widely than to have written well. The burden of supporting the life of imagination had become much too heavy to be borne, not only for individual men but for the age itself. In Buchanan's case the problem resolved itself, according to Shelby, into a crisis of identity. He had by degrees grown less and less sure of who and what he was, what he had been holding out against, what his dedication had been for. The words on the page had been written for another purpose, in the context of expectations relating to a different and older world, and as that world lost its reality, the words lost theirs, until finally they seemed to have been written by someone else or no one. The wilderness, the encroaching nothingness, had won out after all, and Buchanan alone now, his spiritual supplies cut off, the little house turned in fact into an outpost, had at last been forced to succumb, to make his adjustment to the changed conditions, to go over himself to the enemy. Fortunately, he had his considerable reputation to trade on; there was still the salvage value of all that wrecked dedication; and that had bought him his job in Cranton. But the job, Shelby later learned, had cost him his wife, who, with the obstinate idealism so typical of women, had quite rightly come to feel that she had lost the man she had married. With his memory of her—and the memory appeared to have been almost psychotically short— Buchanan had buried all that part of himself which in the beginning she had loved. The humane and brilliant young poet had died in the birth of the imperious critic, the dictatorial editor, the coldly calculating man of knowledge and power. In criticism he seemed to have found not merely a substitute for literature but an escape from it into a realm of absolute and self-regenerating literary value which would be unaffected by the shifting fortunes of history and, unlike literature, would never let him down. In the disciples with whom his editorship surrounded him he seemed to have found slavish replacements as well as convenient scapegoats for his departed friends. In knowledge and power he seemed to have found a kind of perverted outlet for his abandoned creative drives, while in Cranton itself he had quite deliberately constructed a jerry-built academic equivalent of that part of his old life which had been represented by the long evenings of discussion out at the little house. In the loss of his natural community he had, in a sense, founded a community; in the loss of his natural self he had up to a point created a self. But like all substitutes his bore only a superficial resemblance to the real thing. In Cranton he had managed to keep up an appearance at least of his former dedication to the life of the intellect, but the love and the heart were missing, and what had once been a free and passionate exercise of the whole perceiving sensibility had become dogmatized into the meaningless ritual of an arid religion of the head. Ironically enough, he had even, without at all intending to, discovered in Cranton an equivalent of his former isolation and had persevered in the compulsive vocal mannerisms which had been a first symptom of his breakdown within that isolation. He was as fatally cut off from Cranton as he had been from the changing history of his time and from Shelby's father's world, but in Cranton his isolation, rather than being symbolic of his defeat, was looked upon as the very condition of his superiority, and he had there a captive audience who, unlike his wife, were forced to listen to his interminable monologues because of the power he held, or was thought to hold, over them. The transition, however, from Buchanan the poet to Buchanan the man of power was far from complete. There were signs to indicate that he never left off feeling insecure in this strange new Northern world, even after he had come to dominate it, and Shelby at least continued to believe—perhaps because in a sense his own spiritual equilibrium depended on continuing to believe—that Buchanan never left off feeling guilty at having assisted, for reasons of expediency, in the murder of his former self. But all that was of course purely conjectural, a matter of drawing sweeping inferences from evidence that would forever remain pathetically small. For all that was kept well hidden behind the façade of Buchanan's brilliant repertoire of roles—the dissembling mechanisms of his lost and almost vanquished identity.

6.

Shortly after his arrival in Cranton to begin his studies, Shelby had had a single encounter with this newly incarnated Buchanan, and the experience had apparently been shattering. There had been a moment, the barest flicker of an instant, when Shelby felt that something like recognition was beginning to show in Buchanan's face, some slight acknowledging hint that the chain of continuity which bound him to the past and to his old relationship with Shelby had not been altogether severed. There had even been a moment of near panic when Buchanan had seemed to waver anxiously between his new and his former selves and to be uncertain which of them he would use to meet this wholly unprecedented emergency. Then, as though somewhere inside him a button had been pushed, the inscrutable façade swung into place; order was restored, the past brought under control; and Buchanan turned on the special refrigerating apparatus which he had perfected for the terrorization of unwelcome students and underlings— a simple but deadly little device of staring at his victim and saying absolutely nothing until, after searching frantically for words to fill the ghastly silence, the person broke down and fled. Shelby had fled on this occasion, and in the true terror of utter and inexplicable betrayal, but instead of standing in the corridor and trembling with humiliation as the others usually did, he was impelled by the violent force of the shock to return by another route to the scene of his betrayal and to try to comprehend its meaning or at least find some way of justifying its having happened. For the past died hard in him, and he fought against its dying as if he were fighting for his life, which in a sense he was. He accordingly embarked then and there upon the labor of research which ended in the story he had told to Waithe. He turned to knowledge as though it were an FBI file containing the incriminating fingerprints of the secret he sought, as though in facts and ideas understanding could be found for a human condition that, by its very nature, existed on a plane of being which facts and ideas could not begin to reach. He read countless books and articles on philosophy, sociology, history, and the crisis in modern thought. He buried himself in the works of Buchanan's former poet friends turned critics, and felt for a time that he had found there a convincing diagnosis of the spiritual disorder with which Buchanan appeared to be afflicted. He became a subscriber to journals, a clipper of intellectual coupons, a nearly accurate quoter of Kierkegaard and T. E. Hulme. He amassed enough collateral material on the enigma of Buchanan to write a Ph.D. thesis on it, but somewhere along the line he became mesmerized by his own footnotes and by the complication of the process of gathering them. He lost sight of his subject in the intensity of his interest in working it up. Ultimately, he seemed to forget what his subject was, and to find his satisfaction in the sheer breadth of his knowledge of it. At some point knowledge for him seemed to become an end in itself, and it was at that point that knowledge turned into his subject and began to serve him as a substitute for the faith whose loss had driven him to undertake his research in the first place. In knowledge he seemed to find an absolute to which he could give his whole allegiance in the certainty that it would not fail him. It became, in a sense, his compensatory form of religion, just as it had become Buchanan's.

So, ironically enough, it happened that Shelby's effort to find his way back to the meaning of his past with Buchanan brought him into touch with Buchanan once again; his struggle to penetrate the secret of his broken identity with Buchanan ended by making them, at least in this one respect, identical. But it was the new Buchanan Shelby resembled now, not the one with whom he had initially lost contact, and that made the irony almost unbearable. He and this hostile parody of his former friend were bound unwittingly together as fellow manufacturers of false intellectual currency to replace the sound emotional capital they had left behind, and because of that coincidence they were going down together in the destructive element in which they could no longer hold themselves up by the simple strength of their believing hearts. They were both in a way victims of the North, of some defect which rendered them subtly unadaptable to the fate which made them exiles together—exiles from one another, themselves, and the sense they had once had of a common heritage.

But even as he saw this and was touched by it, Waithe continued to be basically unconvinced. Shelby's story still seemed to him much too contrived and melodramatic, much too obviously a product of his over-active imagination of disaster. The clear vision of Buchanan's past which he had hoped to get from it had somehow been lost in the tangle of vaguenesses and circumlocutions through which Shelby had presented it, almost as though in the end Shelby had been trying to hide it from himself, as though the secret it contained had ultimately been more his than Buchanan's. It all reminded Waithe rather offensively of the Negroes dreaming out on Cranton River of a South they had never known, that could never have existed, and trying pathetically to create a substitute for it that would ease the ache of their self-induced nostalgia. He was struck once again by how essential moral forgery is to human life, by how true it is that humankind cannot bear very much reality. But as was the case with the Negroes, reality always kept breaking in: the sounds of bickering behind the shabby façades could not be altogether stilled. One day the illusion would collapse, and the whole sad conspiracy would be exposed to the empty eyes of an indifferent world. Out of the cool calm of a summer afternoon that solitary, deflating voice would once more be raised in the anger of ultimate denunciation. *Tawk, tawk, tawk,* it would cry. *That's awl it evah is or was:* the wax wings of words beating futilely in flight from the awful silence of self-knowledge.

CHAPTER V

1.

WAITHE'S FEELING THAT THE FULL IMPORT OF Shelby's narrative had somehow eluded him—if, indeed, there had been any import to do the eluding—was in no wise mitigated by the young man's subsequent revelation that in the final twelve years of their marriage Buchanan had not once slept with his wife. That singular fact, despite the heavily portentous tones in which it had been announced, seemed to Waithe peculiarly uninstructive, although in view of what he had heard of the ex-Mrs. Buchanan's physical assets, it did give a certain edge to his growing impression that, in the sphere at least of immediate and practical concerns, Buchanan was the undisputed prince of fools. The difficulty, however, from the standpoint of Shelby's narrative was that the event —or, more precisely, its inexplicable absence—antedated by a good eight years Buchanan's self-eviction from the overly mortgaged premises of his former self and, therefore, could not be construed as a symptom either of his monkish determination to give his all to art—for he had even then virtually ceased to write—or of the bankruptcy of his manhood following on the sellout of his art—for it was not until eight years later that a buyer had been found and the sale completed.

The information, for what it was worth, was simply there in the record like a mysterious expenditure in the company accounts, and the only meaning Waithe could see in it was that it made a kind of sickly locker-room joke out of the tense urgency of Mrs. Buchanan's charge that *awl he evah does naow . . . is tawk, tawk, tawk*. That, it appeared, was literally *awl* indeed. It nonetheless did serve to confirm Waithe in his opinion that there was a quality about Buchanan of almost infinitely withheld orgasm, of habitual *coitus interruptus* in the conduct of both spiritual and carnal relations, and that if ever the fertilizing juices of humanity could be said to have backed up in a man, they had backed up in him. It had, in fact, become one of Waithe's secret ambitions at some point to lead Buchanan to the sexual fount and see if he would drink, but he was reasonably certain that the experiment would fail miserably. Not only had Buchanan never shown signs of having any thirst that five tall glasses of bourbon could not appease, but the prolonged sexual drought in Cranton had resulted in an acute shortage of founts. One might even have concluded—as indeed Waithe already had—that the drought, by its very length and severity, had so upset the rational order of things that Buchanan had himself become a sexual fount for the women of Cranton, the chief source of irrigation for the arid lands of their erotic fantasies, and was thereby effectively protected from ever having to prove his potency in bed. For he irrigated, as it were, by hypnosis, played incubus to their Trilby, and his entire attraction rested on the fact that he was available to them only in their dreams. His was the one heft not taken in the yellow wood of their parched imaginations, and so they sighingly assumed that it would make all the difference.

But as Waithe had predicted, such illusions had sooner or later to submit to the test of reality, and all that was necessary in the case of this one was to discover a fount inviting enough to arouse in Buchanan the proper thirst. Since the local supply was so low, it would probably be necessary to import one from out of town, and as it happened, the opportunity to do just that presented itself much sooner than Waithe could have expected. It came in the form of an invitation solicitously rendered to Dorothy Murchison to spend a year in Cranton and give a series of the coveted Matilda Makepeace Willycombe lectures in classical literature. Dorothy was an exemplary candidate for both the lectureship and Waithe's little experiment. On the academic side she was the author of three definitive works on the literary culture of Greece and Rome, and held all the requisite degrees as well as a high French military decoration for having allowed herself to be parachuted repeatedly into France during the dangerous days of the German occupation. Her qualifications for bed were no less impressive, although their precise extent and nature seemed destined to remain one of the closely guarded secrets of the war. She was known, however, by just about everyone except the Cranton board of trustees to be as well and as widely slept with as Buchanan was not, and Waithe had learned from direct personal experience that she could be trusted to try to seduce every man she met, especially if he constituted the clear challenge to her powers that Buchanan did. Perhaps because of her wartime training she was particularly attracted to men of eminence and authority. She took them to bed the way less resourceful operatives might have rifled safes and photographed documents—as though she still interpreted with literal strictness her former role of undercover agent. Every man of this type seemed to represent to her another oakleaf cluster for her Legion of Dishonor, and a catalogue of the names of those with whom she had thus far assuaged her patriotic hungers would have read like a roster of the Allied and Axis General Staffs combined with the male membership of the National Institute of Arts and Letters. Waithe had met her in a slit trench in Normandy, and their acquaintanceship had been consummated to the accompaniment of the shelling of Cherbourg—an activity which she had likened, between moans, to the siege of Troy. The affair had continued through most of the principal bombardments of the European campaign and had finally come to an end in a Piccadilly hotel room on a very warm August afternoon when she had decided, with a bleary but dispassionate eye on the looming civilian horizon, that Waithe, while *weeley a tewibwy sveet booye*, would never, never be either eminent or authoritative. He also had absolutely nothing to give her except his hopelessly unclassified heart and soul, which, like everything else about him, had long since been bared to her methodical but increasingly unrewarding inspection, and no longer held any secrets worth radioing home about. She clearly needed far wider scope for her investigative sexuality than Waithe was able to provide, and so he lost her in the year of the war's end to an exiled Balkan king whom she suspected of plotting the golf-club assassination of General Eisenhower. But that was in another theater of operations, and besides Buchanan was a different matter altogether. Not only did he qualify handsomely on the score of eminence and authority, but he was a triple-padlocked, armor-plated, spy-proof file cabinet of top-secret information. Breaking into him would be as excitingly difficult as burgling the Pentagon, and Waithe knew that Dorothy would not fail to recognize him as the most challenging assignment of her long and distinguished career.

The problem of course was to bring them together, and this Waithe managed simply by calling them both up and inviting them over to his house to meet each other. Dorothy was delighted to hear from him and proceeded to make peculiar labial-sounding noises into her end of the wire—noises which Waithe had long ago learned to interpret as being the result of an obscure foreign accent which she seemed to have acquired while growing up on a chicken farm in northern Idaho. Buchanan for his part made gruffling and whuffling noises, punctuated by long stretches of bad *cameriere* Italian acquired on his last Guggenheim, but Waithe gathered that he would come provided he could be assured of adequate transport.

2.

The night Waithe chose for the confrontation was a pleasantly warm one in early spring. The flowers around his little house were just coming into bloom; the crickets and tree toads in the swampy woods across the road had resumed their rhythmic seasonal telegraphy; a soft wind of the type Buchanan was certain to compare at interminable length with the Italian sirocco blew in placid gusts in a direction which Waithe inferred from the odor of apple blossoms to be toward rather than away from the river. The bluish glow of the fires from Cranton's neighboring valley of ashes flickered with a funereal coziness on the eastern horizon, and as he drove in to pick up his guests, Waithe could scarcely suppress the hackneyed thought that all the forces of nature seemed to be conspiring together to create the most favorable circumstances possible for the success of his first venture into pimpery.

The lights were all on in Buchanan's ground-floor apartment when Waithe drew up in front of it, and he could see through the big study window the figure of the great man carefully posed in his old leather armchair, a heavy volume held ostentatiously open in one hand, a cigarette propped prissily in the other, looking as though he were sitting for his portrait to the whole wondering night world of Cranton. As Waithe entered, the book was thrust forward so that he would be sure to see the title (it was *The Vatican Index of the Canonical Orders of the Medieval Church*); Buchanan heaved ponderously to his feet; hands were shaken; there was the usual awkward problem of what to do with one's eyes. While Buchanan busied himself in the bathroom, Waithe wandered about picking up and laying down objects and leafing through the latest issues of the *Kenyon, Sewanee, Partisan, Hudson, Yale*, and *Cranton Reviews*. Finally Buchanan reappeared, and with a quasi-courteous *Sir*, which meant that he was bestowing upon Waithe the privilege of preceding him out the door, he followed Waithe down the walk to the car, and they drove over to get Dorothy. She emerged almost at once, still zipping up her dress, planted a wide-open and very breathy kiss on Waithe's mouth, shook Buchanan's hand over the front seat, and climbed into the back beside him. For a while they drove in what Waithe took to be a maneuvering silence. Then Buchanan interrupted it with the information—which it took him the entire length of the return trip to give full expositional form to—that the wind then blowing was very similar, particularly in its texture and harmonics, to the Italian sirocco which he had first experienced while sitting one evening on the terrace of the Hotel Panoramica in Fiello del Adorechia on the Lago Frindisquomo. He had just returned, he said, from an afternoon of studying some allegedly Etruscan frescoes which had recently been uncovered on the ancient walls of the Chiesa Felichimare, and he and the headwaiter had had a spirited argument over their age. *Uno mille tre cento,* Buchanan said he had insisted. *No, no, mi rincresce, signor,* the headwaiter had replied, *ma sono proprio due mille quattro cento. Due mille quattro cento! Baaah,* Buchanan had said, *è non possible! Baaah! Si, si,* the headwaiter had said, *sono due mille quattro cento! Waaahooo,* Buchanan bellowed out of the back seat. *Due mille quattro cento, due mille quattro cento,* he mimicked in a fast falsetto. *BOORAH!* Then it sounded very much as though he said, *Boorah, quandichi il a povono BOOOORAH!* But Waithe, who at that moment was engaged in frantically wrenching the wheel to avoid hitting a rabbit which had run out in front of the car and sat down, did not hear how the argument ended, although there was a good deal of verbal activity going on in the back seat, and he did hear Dorothy say in a small, coy tone that passed with her for coquetry, *Ay do not theenk you war werry nahayce to heem.* Then they turned into Waithe's driveway.

It was in this mood of gentle conversational pleasantry that the evening began. Nothing, at least at the outset, could have been more charming and relaxed, more completely in keeping with the seditious character of Waithe's hopes, if not his expectations, than the occasion promised to be. Buchanan and Dorothy seemed to have taken to each other at once. They sat together on the big living-room sofa as totally absorbed in themselves as if they had been a pair of veteran actors playing a homey domestic scene in the middle of a stage. Buchanan

of course did most of the talking, and Dorothy listened and
nodded and smiled and occasionally giggled. All she needed
was a pile of knitting in her lap, and all he needed was pipe
and slippers. And the elements, the normally refractory props
of arrogant destiny and the higher cosmos, co-operated with
a serene willingness that could scarcely have been achieved
with pulleys and wires. The soft wind blew obligingly through
the open windows, gently swaying and fattening the curtains,
lifting every now and then a corner of Dorothy's skirt, easing
out of place a single strand of her hair. Buchanan leaned
majestically back, his tie slightly askew, one arm flopped over
behind the sofa, and seemed to swell and exhale in rhythm
with the wind, obviously luxuriating in his audience and his
brilliance, time itself seeming to hang on his every word and
to hold its breath with his. It was all very blowy and peaceful
and springlike, almost as though they were on board a ship in
a tropical sea, and Waithe did little but hover deferentially,
an imaginary towel on his arm, and keep the glasses filled.
Buchanan was in top form that evening. Charm shone forth
from him as if his customary spleen had become radioactive.
He even smiled and showed his teeth—a phenomenon Waithe
could not remember having witnessed before. Once or twice
he even laughed aloud—mostly, to be sure, at his own clever-
nesses—but for the first time his laugh did not sound like a
wounded bull elephant charging its assailant through the tall
grass of Kenya. He told stories about Italy, and some of them
were almost funny. He was dazzlingly epigrammatic on all of
Dorothy's favorite subjects—Homer and Vergil, Sophocles and
Aeschylus, Tacitus and Thucydides. He did a wonderful imitation of T. S. Eliot reciting "The Hollow Men" down the
drainpipe of a Soho pub, and he even lay on the floor and did

a passable imitation of Dylan Thomas reciting "Trees" on the floor of the White Horse Tavern. Through it all Dorothy sat like a little girl at her first circus, her eyes sparkling, a pretty flush in her cheeks, clapping her hands in gay delight at the performance.

Just how long this went on Waithe could not have said, nor was he at all sure just when it was that a change came over everything, and the whole room suddenly began to rush and whirl as though shaken into panic by some dark reminder of its complicity with fate. He knew only that he had been back and forth from the kitchen countless times, and that on one of those times he seemed to have stepped off into another dimension and floundered about for an incalculable while in infinity, for when he returned, it was as though a year had passed. The wind had grown blustery and belligerent and blew through the room like a typhoon. The curtains stood out from the windows like battle pennants at a medieval tourney-at-arms; lamps swayed and rattled on their stands; magazines madly leafed themselves on tables; a picture fell with a clatter from the wall. All the objects in the room appeared to be hanging suspended several inches off the floor and waiting to be blown out of the house on the next blast. It had turned so abruptly cold that Waithe wondered irrationally for a second whether he had left the refrigerator open. Only Buchanan and Dorothy seemed unaffected by the prevailing disorder. They sat as Waithe had left them, although now they looked oddly pulled together and prim, as if they had been quietly sipping tea in a Victorian drawing room and someone had just made an indecent remark. It even occurred to Waithe with a swift swelling of hope that he might have interrupted a necking session and perhaps ought to withdraw discreetly.

But then he sensed that they had been quarreling. Buchanan was in the middle of one of his famous badgering performances, and the object was evidently Dorothy's accent, on which he was concentrating with a hypnotic force that would have done credit to a Russian wolfhound. She, in turn, was looking at him with the stunned and baffled expression of a cornered mouse confronting a boa constrictor. They were both totally oblivious of everything around them—of the raging wind, the insane confusion of the room, even of Waithe himself as he sat down in a chair facing them. He had the feeling that he could have started taking off his clothes and they would not have noticed. After a moment he became so convinced of their indifference, their utter remoteness from the scene, that he had the impulse to get up and go get a pad and pencil and take notes, for the performance was excellent, and the dialogue —or, more correctly, the monologue, since it was mostly Buchanan's—much too good to be lost to posterity. In fact, he did get up and go get a pad and pencil and take notes, but they were still oblivious.

Buchanan had the idea that Dorothy really had no accent, having bullied it out of her that she had grown up on a chicken farm in northern Idaho. He insisted that she was putting it all on for his benefit, and to test this hypothesis he was having her pronounce certain words, and she was doing her best to comply. *Very*, he would say. *Werry*, she would answer. *Critical*, he would say. *Creeteecal*, she would answer. *Woman*, he would say. *Vooman*, she would answer. *Bitch*, he would say. *Beetch*, she would answer. *Slut*, he would say. *Slurt*, she would answer. *Tramp*, he would say. *Trahmp*, she would answer. *Strumpet*, he would say. *Stroompet*, she would answer. *Whore*, he would say. *Whoor*, she would answer. Finally he gave it up and began with a pretense of playfulness to pinch and twist her arm—on the theory, he said, that people in enough pain will sooner or later react in their own language. *Does that hurt?* he kept asking her. When she made no reply, he would pinch and twist harder and say, *All right then. Does that hurt? No? Well then. Does THAT hurt?* Dorothy was trying desperately to cope with the situation, grimly shaking her head each time he applied the pressure. But her lips were shut tight against the pain; her face was very pale; and she was obviously on the verge of tears. Waithe realized that it was probably about time for him to intervene, but the effect of the drinks combined with his sense of the hazy remoteness of everything that was going on prevented him from doing so. Buchanan and Dorothy still seemed to him like actors performing on a stage—abstract, pretending creatures without flesh and blood and emotions. At any moment now the curtain would descend, and they would come out holding hands and advance into the footlights and bow and smile at him. He was even tempted suddenly to break into applause and only just managed to restrain himself when he saw his hands raised before him, recognized them as his own, and watched them begin to come together. Instead, he got to his feet, gathered up the empty glasses, and went into the kitchen, firmly intending to make more drinks. Some time later he was vaguely aware of himself leaning against the wall of the basement bathroom and urinating for an incredible while into the sink. When finally he ascended the stairs, he heard the heavy roar of rain; the wind was raging through the house with cyclone force; and he hurried to shut the windows. By the time he had finished, Buchanan and Dorothy were standing in the hall, obviously wanting to leave, and he was conscious of the startling cold of the rain on his face as he ran with them to the car.

The drive back to town was like a descent by two-door sedan into some Poean maelstrom. The rain blew in great splattering gusts against the car, and the wind seemed to heave at it as though straining with everything it had to tip them all into the ditch. Through the river of water that streamed down the windshield, Waithe could just make out the bottomless black of the road ahead and the hovering gray ghosts of trees standing on either side, their wet limbs and trunks seeming to exude an ominous mistiness that reminded him of the haunted graveyards in old horror films. Every now and then immense flashes of lightning would brighten the landscape to a ghastly atomic whiteness, and these would be followed by heavy, earth-shuddering spasms and booms as though somewhere not very far off a city were being devastated by an enemy missile bombardment. But through and above it all, like the raving of some mad fiddleless Nero, came the sound of Buchanan's voice keening and lowing and expostulating out of the back seat. Because of the noise of the rain and wind it was impossible for Waithe to tell at first what language or languages he was speaking, or whether, in fact, it was language. At moments it sounded as though he simply had his mouth open and the wind was howling through the caverns of his head. At other moments it was like a catechism or chant or an esoteric imprecation being hurled out upon the perverse intractability of the elements. But then in the intervals between thunderclaps Waithe was able to hear snatches of what he took to be song or recitation, interspersed with long passages of mumbling monologue. The name of Norman Douglas came floating through the car like a drowned body that had just become untangled from a mass of underwater vegetation. Then Buchanan was chanting in a very loud voice, *There was an old woman from Wheeling/ Who had a peculiar feeling.* Dorothy at that point seemed to scream out, although whether in ecstasy or pain Waithe was unable to tell. Buchanan, however, seemed to have recovered his wounded bull-elephant laugh, and that for some time dominated all other sound. Then Buchanan was telling about a period in his youth when he had been a purveyor of certain female phallic instruments smuggled in from Cuba, and had worked as a bouncer in an establishment where there were two ladies and a swan who put on nightly exhibitions before an audience of men who commonly gave themselves up to behavior of a somewhat intimate nature. Waithe wondered for an instant whether this could have occurred before or after Buchanan came into Shelby's life, but then he decided that he had no more reason for believing this story than he had for believing Shelby's—far less, in fact, for Buchanan had a whole range of outrageous lies to choose a past from, while Shelby had merely exaggerated certain aspects of a past which had unquestionably chosen him. Then Waithe felt a draft of cold air against the back of his neck as someone rolled one of the rear windows down, and he half turned in his seat just as Buchanan stuck his head and shoulders out into the storm and began yelling MOOOHA, MOOOOOOHAAA, NOOOOMENOOOOM, MOOOOHAAA. *Ahbate,* said Dorothy, AHHHBAAAATE, Buchanan shouted, still hanging out of the window. This was followed by a series of wild guffaws and giggles; Dorothy screamed again; there was a sound of scuffling and finally of the window being rolled up. Then all was very quiet until they stopped at the curb in front of Buchanan's apartment.

The storm had become by that time a steady drenching down-pour, and Waithe was reluctant at first to accept Buchanan's invitation to come in for a nightcap. But finally, after deciding that he could get no wetter than he already was, he acquiesced and ran with the others through the rain to the door.

Inside, Buchanan lighted a fire and made drinks; Dorothy dried her hair on a towel; and Waithe went off to the bath-room, where he admired at considerable length Buchanan's new collection of pornographic prints smuggled in from Pompeii. By the time he returned, Dorothy had taken off her wet dress and was wearing an old Japanese robe of Buchanan's; her hair was loose and damp and falling on her shoulders; and she and Buchanan were sitting close together on the sofa reading the *Purgatorio* aloud to each other in the original Italian. Waithe settled himself in a chair before the fire, sipped his drink, and did some more leafing through maga-zines. A very long time seemed to pass, during which the voices droned on from the sofa, ice rattled periodically in glasses, the burning logs blazed and crackled, and Waithe read a heavily vituperative attack on Lionel Trilling by a former disciple, and a poem about the New England of Robert Frost by a former member of the Communist party. Finally it came over him that Dorothy showed every sign of planning to spend what was left of the night, so he got up and made some excuse about having an eight-o'clock class the next day. On the way out he thought he detected an odd expression in Buchanan's eyes, but could make nothing of it except that it vaguely re-sembled the kind of look that might have passed between con-spirators meeting at a public reception in a building which they were shortly going to dynamite. As he went down the front walk to his car, Waithe realized that he had no feeling of triumph over the apparent success of his little experiment: he felt only tired and rather baffled. He paused for a moment to turn this over in his mind and noticed suddenly that the rain had stopped and that dark clouds were moving very fast across the face of a hazy, sickly-looking moon. While he was staring up into the sky, he heard for the first time from the apartment behind him that singular sound which he was later able to identify as Buchanan's gigantic howl.

3.

It came as no particular surprise to Waithe that he never learned precisely what took place after he left that night. He had lived long enough in Cranton to know that the most crucial events could occur there and leave no trace whatever, almost as though any fugitive drama that happened to sneak into town was at once sneaked out again so that it could be brought to justice in some other town that had nothing to lose by the publicity. He also know—or thought he knew—the principal parties to the crime—if crime was the right word for whatever it was that had occurred. Buchanan was obviously the sort of man to whom nothing, properly speaking, ever happened: he only happened to other people like an act of God or a fatal fall in the bathtub. Experience was an offense to both his private fastidiousness and his public arrogance, and Buchanan never took offense; he only offended. In the case of Dorothy there was a much wider range of unpredictability. Everything, improperly speaking, happened to her; she *never* happened to other people, unless a person chanced to be male and a sentimentalist or male and drunk. Still, Waithe was again not particularly surprised that she acted, when he next

saw her, as though nothing whatever had occurred that night
—assuming of course that something *had,* and that they had
not simply sat up all night reading Dante with Buchanan
howling at intervals just out of wild delight at the verisimili-
tude of the portrait of hell. There was, first of all, the fact that,
in spite of her almost professional promiscuity, Dorothy had
like every professional her own statute of ethical limitations,
her own method of paying out blackmail to what was left of
her conscience. She did not wear her conquests on her garter
belt like scalps, if only because the war had taught her that
victory is as much a matter of available equipment as it is of
personal virtue, and while there might be grave doubts about
her virtue, there could be none whatever about the availability
of her equipment. She had, after all, her modesty. Then in the
case of her supposed conquest of Buchanan, there was the
second very real possibility that she had been as taken with
him as presumably she had been taken by him. He had obviously puzzled her, fascinated her, frightened her—had perhaps in the end even blundered upon the bottommost secret
of her nature, which was that she invited and enjoyed abuse.
The overt sadist in Buchanan might have responded to the
concealed masochist in her with such high satisfaction to them
both that she had been inspired—as for different reasons
Shelby had been inspired—to a discreet reticence about their
relationship that had positively been sealed in blood. At the
climactic moment of Heaven only knew what supreme in-
dignity visited upon her by a leering, hot-eyed Buchanan, she
could easily have become another stockholder in his company.
In that event, the howl that Waithe had heard could well
have been Buchanan's way of proclaiming the bargain successfully negotiated, and Dorothy's silence could be construed as

her way of protecting her investment. For Dorothy not only invited abuse; she kept it stored in her bosom next to her bleeding heart and would take it out on rainy days and dream over it, as though it were a faded snapshot of an old sweetheart killed at the Somme.

Then there was the third possibility, which Waithe happened to know was also a fact, that Dorothy was something of a pathological liar—an attribute which had largely accounted for her brilliant success as a secret agent if not as a classics scholar. But lying operated with her in more than the usual single direction: it was able not only to fabricate something that had obviously never happened, but it could wipe out of existence something that just as obviously had. When the lying mood was on her, Dorothy was quite capable of calling people up in the middle of the night and moaning that she was *tewibwy, tewibwy dayprayzzed* and would shortly be killing herself if they did not rush over at once and prevent her. When they arrived, half expecting to have to cut her down from the chandelier, they would find her in bed placidly eating a chocolate-covered cherry, and she would look up at them out of her big startled-fawn eyes and say, *Oooh, how werry nahayce of you to come to zee me.*

For these and other reasons Dorothy was a deeply untrustworthy witness, and not the least of the other reasons was that, on top of everything else, she was a cliché, and a far worse one than Shelby had been. She was the very type of the beautiful, hard-drinking, inveterately bedridden women over whom private eyes were perpetually kicking desk drawers open and shut in cheap novels, the sort of woman whose testimony would never have been admitted into the record of any court of however worldly judgment, regardless of the pleasure the judge might have derived from looking all day at her legs. It did not matter, therefore, what she said or might have said or did not say about the events of that night with Buchanan: Waithe would not have believed her anyway. In fact, it came as a considerable relief to him that she had decided to say nothing, for it saved him the trouble of having to disbelieve her and then of having to imagine, laboriously and on his own hook with her babbling tritely away before him, what conceivably *could* have occurred. Still, his relief was by no means so complete or assured that it did not benefit immeasurably from the fact that he found ample additional evidence for her untrustworthiness in the events that followed, especially in her conduct of the Matilda Makepeace Willycombe lectures, at at least one of which—the first—Waithe made a special point of being present.

4.

Dorothy made her Cranton lecture debut clothed in a black and very low-cut evening gown beneath which she obviously had nothing on whatever. In the bright glare of the reading lamp her arms and shoulders shone with an almost strip-tease whiteness against the black, and her large breasts bulged threateningly out upon the desk at which she sat as though at any moment they were going to pop up over their parapet of silk and start cannonading the audience. The lecture room was filled nearly to capacity by a carefully selected crowd composed of the more favored inmates of Buchanan's little kennel of contrite young men, two or three ex-Willycombe performers (of whom Miriam Hornblower was one), and a few haggard-faced professors from the Cranton Classics Department. Waithe located a seat in the rear of the room, and during the initial moments of the proceedings lost himself in contemplation of the assorted backs of heads and in making visual assessments of their cranial hefts. An alarming proportion of those present appeared to be afflicted with premature baldness and microcephalia; dandruff lay like scattered minuscule snowflakes on several coat collars; and Waithe had a bad moment of vertiginous transport when he imagined himself whooping and hallooing down those powdery slopes in the body of a ski-shod fly. Then Buchanan was making various introductory remarks which sounded, from where Waithe was sitting, as though they were being delivered through a poor telephone connection by a defective tape-recorder located in Somaliland. Then Dorothy began to speak, or at least her lips began to move, and words of a sort seemed to be coming out. Waithe strained forward in his chair and managed to understand her to say that Plato wanted to expel all poets from the republic because they threatened to seduce the sister of his son-in-law—although, of course, what she actually said was *Playdo wahnded to expail all poeds frahm the ray*PUB*lique baycauwse zay tretened to trahduce za zeeeztaym uvreez*-SOHN *oonlawr*. But she kept fading out like a weak shortwave signal, and Waithe had to keep leaning forward to tune her in again. Then for a moment or so she would come back loud and clear. Then, inexplicably, there would be nothing but a low mumble like the sound given off by a hive of agitated bees. Finally, the effect regularized itself into a system of alternating coherences and peculiar, untranslatable noises. Single words and phrases would float dreamily back to Waithe over the ranked heads of the audience, and these would be surrounded by long ectoplasmic passages of incomprehensibility. *Ay theenk*, she seemed to be saying, *eet eesr puttra-*

simspaflismurtinflus Peendar wars a werry Osteer writar and apalafustus zis Meestair Leeveengstun cratititsmish pairhahps coodave mayda betair trahnslazshun. Ay raymembair wan ay warse a girl you mahyt zay EEN-CON-SEE-QUEN-SHEE-ALEE *eengrossed een Ahreestophahnees thayre warse a theeowree zat da Frauwgs war extuelle ah folk fantassee uv schmelinkmechim or da older hwerthsunix, although ay do not eentairally ahgree....* The strain after a while became too much for Waithe, and he let his exhausted attention wander once more among the assembled backs of heads, where it languished for several seconds until suddenly rejuvenated by a curious fact. Although many of the heads showed obvious symptoms of having succumbed in the fierce battle for understanding, certain others were not only still alive and alert but even nodding eagerly in evident agreement with just about everything that Dorothy was saying. Waithe's first thought was that the trouble all along might have been that he was losing his hearing. Then he realized that the nodders were all Buchanan's young men, whose arduous Pavlovean training had long ago conditioned them to nod agreeably at everything said under the proper academic auspices whether or not they heard or understood it, for one never knew in Cranton when yesterday's incomprehensibility might turn out to be today's profundity.

It was, of course, from among the nodders that the bulk of the questions came in the discussion period that followed the lecture. One young man, who looked as though he had sat for the portrait of "His Master's Voice," got up and asked Dorothy what she thought of the relation between Eastern meditative art, as described in Foucher's *Iconographie Bouddhique,* and the decidedly empiric rationale of Polygnotus.

Dorothy replied that there was no relation whatever, and the young man sat down under Buchanan's grimly executionary stare. Another young man, whom Waithe recognized as belonging to the English Department, next arose, and to the accompaniment of a great deal of squirming and wagging, launched into profuse apologies for being about to intrude, as he put it, his big toe into Dorothy's domain. Dorothy looked at him as though he were suggesting that she participate in something perverted, but all he wanted to know was whether truth and art were not for the Greeks dialectically opposed concepts. She was rescued from having to answer, however, by still another young man who asked the second young man to define his terms. Some time and several definitions later, Miriam Hornblower stood up and announced through her customary ghastly smile, which was like the first thing you saw when you opened a grave, that *heh* Molière *heh* in *Tartuffe heh* brought *heh* the art *heh* of *l'exaggeration heh juste* to final *heh* perfection *heh*, while the *reductio ad heh absurdum heh* of the Aristotelean *heh* concept of "truthfulness *heh* to type" *heh* is achieved *heh* not, as is commonly *heh* supposed *heh*, in Sophocles' Electra *heh* but in Euripides' *heh*. Dorothy, it appeared, had said that it is achieved in Sophocles'. *Ja,* said Miriam's companion, the drama critic Rachel Fliegelheimer, *vat you mean iss dot Molière turned Aristotle oppseit town, vile de Grrrrrreek teater of Eurrrrrripides iss alvays turning him townseit opp like Haaaaaaygel und Marks.* There was a great deal of affirmative nodding at this, followed by a moment of excited muttering between Miriam and Rachel. The young man with the big toe leaned over to them and apparently said something searching, for they all tittered, and Rachel made an entry in the big black notebook she always carried. Then Buchanan rose from his moderator's chair on the platform beside Dorothy, favored the assemblage with his most beneficent, head-patting expression, asked if there were any further questions, and said that if there were not, he would save his own question concerning the mimetic forms of Attic farce until a later occasion. He then proclaimed the meeting adjourned.

5.

At the traditional post-first Willycombe lecture party held for the speaker and a few selected guests at Buchanan's apartment, Dorothy was of course the center of a pressing mob of stuttering and earnestly finger-stabbing interrogators. For some reason, no one ever seemed able in Cranton to work up the courage necessary to articulation without first creating a diversionary display of calisthenics, and it had not been very long before that Anthony Marsh, the most athletic articulator of them all, had rather badly dislocated his shoulder while asking someone his equivalent of "Read any good books lately?" The result was that the group around Dorothy looked from where Waithe was sitting as though they were raining blows down on top of her head. But from time to time, as people came and went, he could see her standing stanch and unscathed in the middle of it all and making her replies in a firm, high voice which seemed to him to be delivering itself like a stuck, do-it-yourself language record of an endless series of *ay theenks* and *pairhaps's*. As the party got under way, however, and glasses were emptied and refilled, Waithe noticed that her voice grew steadily louder and somewhat combative, and following whatever she said there would be frequent startled silences accompanied by a nervous shifting of feet among the interrogators and an occasional embarrassed "Oh, I *say*" from some of the more delicate members of the British scholarship contingent. But Waithe was himself engaged—or, more correctly, being engaged—in an interminable conversation with Rachel Fliegelheimer, who seemed not to be hearing a word he was saying, since what she was saying interested her far more, and that kept him occupied for a very long time, during which he lost sight of Dorothy altogether. When next he saw her again—Rachel having finally drifted off with the young man with the big toe—she was sprawled in a chair abandoned by everyone, her eyes shut, mouth open, legs stretched limply before her like a pair of overripe bananas, completely passed out. Waithe managed with a good deal of effort to get her to her feet, and she stood swaying against him and mumbling to herself until suddenly and surprisingly she woke up and gurgled as though she had been fed too much Clapp's Baby Food. Someone had put on a jazz record, and she insisted that she wanted to dance with her *Inglés*—a reference to a bit of amorous make-believe they had once indulged in during their slit-trench and sleeping-bag days together. So they went round and round, staggering rather badly and bumping into furniture, she hanging onto his neck like a drowning child and breathing into his face bilious hot wafts of bourbon and ginger ale and humming sad, off-key snatches of old music-hall songs which she had boozily dredged up out of her memory of wartime London. It came over Waithe that he remembered them himself, and he realized with a certain disgust that he was humming along with her. He even found himself trying to recall the names of the places they had been when they had first heard them. But after a moment he noticed that the music had stopped, and someone was putting on another record. Then someone else was dancing with Dorothy, and Miriam Hornblower came up with that grin from the grave, and he was standing there looking at Miriam and feeling as though there was something he had just been about to say which she had rudely interrupted. But since he could not think what it might have been, he grinned back at Miriam and wandered off into the next room, where he found Buchanan holding court before a little assemblage of young wives and disconsolate-looking young men.

Buchanan was evidently in the midde of his favorite party game, and even though Waithe knew the routine pretty thoroughly—having himself been taken in by it more than once—he still derived a certain grim satisfaction from watching it being worked on the kind of purposely unsuspecting, almost willfully credulous audience which it always seemed to attract. The truth was, of course, that the audience was never in the least unsuspecting: in this case there was scarcely a person in the room who was not as much in the know as Waithe was. Yet the whole point and viciousness of the game consisted precisely in the fact that this did not matter in the slightest, if only because no one present could afford to let it matter. Like compulsive roulette players, they all knew down in their secret hearts that they hadn't a chance in a thousand; yet they were all held there, starey-eyed, sweaty-palmed, and helpless, by the faint possibility that tonight just might be the night for that old number to come up. And Buchanan knew with equal certainty that they knew: that was the measure of his viciousness, just as his ownership of the casino was the measure of his power. He knew, and the knowledge added that slight but psychologically monstrous fillip that gave the game its peculiar sadistic fascination. As a result of his Pavlovean researches, to say nothing of the contributions he had personally made to the refined science of the third degree and the academic brain wash, Buchanan was well acquainted with the workings of the ever-hopeful, it-is-out-of-our-hands faculty of the human mind, and knew that he could tease, tantalize, and ultimately derange it just as effectively no matter how many times he rang the same bell, pushed the same button, or probed the same nerve center. The victim would always salivate on schedule whether you shoved food at him or not, and he would probably salivate all the harder if there was a chance that you after all might not. The trick of course was to keep the victim ravenous, and that Buchanan took care to do by passing a slab of fresh meat under his nose from time to time and even letting him take an occasional bite, just so that he would not forget the taste. The fresh meat in this case was the slight but still tangible evidence that the game *did* now and then have behind it a serious purpose, that it was not after all always a game. There had been those who had distinctly profited by it, or at least there were said to have been, and it was on the basis of this that Buchanan kept his victims off guard and continuing to salivate obligingly whenever he decided that he wanted them to.

It was really a very simple game, and the idea for it had obviously occurred to Buchanan as one of the several possible variants of the old false-publication gambit with which on dull days he liked to amuse himself at the expense of his young assistants on *The Cranton Review*. His customary method was to pick an innocuous and preferably flagging moment in the conversation and begin with an apparent air of the utmost sincerity to describe a letter which had come in the mail that morning. The letter posed problems of such a complex and delicate nature that he felt he had to solicit the advice of his audience as to how he might best proceed. It appeared that Harvard was thinking of creating a special new professorship in contemporary American literature and had asked him to submit a list of possible candidates and to serve on the selection committee should the plan materialize. The salary would of course be high, but then so would the standards of qualification. The letter had specified that the incumbent should be a young man of between thirty-five and forty or forty and forty-five (depending on the age of most of the young men present), be currently on the staff of a major Eastern university such as Cranton, be the author of an original work in the field, published or, he would add significantly, eminently publishable, and be at least a fairly regular contributor of scholarly articles and monographs to such magazines as—and he would name all the magazines to which he knew the young men present were fairly regular contributors.

A charged silence would as a rule follow this kind of announcement, during which wives would look with defiant and distinctly nasty expectancy at husbands, and husbands would seem to look nervously inside themselves as though checking to see if their spiritual zippers had come open. One could almost hear popping around the room like a string of ganglionic firecrackers the sudden fevered recollections of all those unpublished—and perhaps not even *eminently* publishable, let alone original—works locked away in bottom dresser drawers, and each man would struggle to make a fast eleventh-hour calculation of where he stood in the abstruse algebraic hierarchy of Buchanan's favor. Finally, some tormented soul, who had nothing to lose but his head, would inquire gaspingly what salary was being contemplated. Buchanan would of course name the largest figure within the limits of plausibility that he could think of, and there would be more looks and recollections, this time even nastier and more fevered. Then Buchanan would ask the young man who had spoken if he were by any chance a specialist in some such unlikely subject as the shorter poems of D. H. Lawrence, knowing full well that the young man was not. The letter, he would say, had indicated that they particularly wanted a specialist in that subject, and he would add, as if thinking out loud, that there *was*, after all, so-and-so (a person widely recognized as being an absolute incompetent) who just might qualify for the job. At once someone would frantically point out that so-and-so was positively not a specialist in that subject. Buchanan would reply that he knew that, but that so-and-so *was* between thirty-five and forty, currently on the staff of such-and-such, and a fairly regular contributor to this-and-that—this time naming none of the magazines to which the young men present were fairly regular contributors.

His standard practice then was to launch abruptly into one of his interminable pedantic monologues, leaving his audience stranded and panting on the very brink of oasis, but not knowing whether what they had seen was real or a mirage. For Waithe, however, the performance was a very old movie indeed, and he felt no desire to sit through it again, even though he did always enjoy the consummate bastardliness with which Buchanan played his part. He therefore went back into the other room and pushed through the crowd of people in search of Dorothy. At first he thought she must have left, for he could find her nowhere in the crowd, and she was not among the casualties who lay scattered around on the furniture in various attitudes of stupefied inaction. But then in one dim corner of the room he found her standing in the arms of the young man with the big toe, tenderly engaged in kissing the soft underbelly of his chin. Although there was no longer any music, they appeared to be dancing or, at any rate, moving and swaying about. But as Waithe approached, he saw that she was blindly and amorously drunk and that the young man was trying with acute embarrassment to fend her off, keep her quiet, and at the same time hold her up. He looked at Waithe with touching but stalwartly silent appeal, and for a long moment Waithe fought against the temptation simply to leave them there unrescued on their little desert isle, panting for salvation like Buchanan's victims while the awful realization of the world's indifference broke over them like undrinkable surf. But something else inside him, some innate but—he knew—strictly reflex sympathy for human distress, prompted him at last to launch a boat and pick up the survivors. He took Dorothy by one arm, instructed the young man to take her by the other, and together they got her headed out the door, down the front walk, and bundled into the back of Waithe's car.

During the drive to her apartment Dorothy kept up an incessant babble in some drunken unknown tongue of which Waithe could understand nothing except what he took to be the word *bahstahd* being repeated at regular intervals over and over as though it formed part of some abstruse litany or catechism. It reminded him a little of the sound Buchanan had made from the back seat on the night of his first meeting with Dorothy, but this had behind it some morosely sustained insistence, some steadfast singularity of purpose, however indecipherable, which the other had not had. At times it seemed to attain a quality of pitch and tonal structure approaching that of song—a sad, lamenting Ophelia's song. At other times it seemed to rise through scales as yet undiscovered by music and to reach a crisis of volume that ravaged the air like a witch's yowl of vengeance. But when at last they arrived at the apartment, it died away into a babble once more, and Ophelia and the witch became simply a helpless woman, pale, disheveled, but still somehow beautiful, conversing incoherently with herself in some hallucinatory drawing room to which she alone seemed to hold the key.

Waithe and the young man got Dorothy out of the car and half carried, half dragged her over the sidewalk to the front door. On the stairs leading up to her rooms Waithe pulled and the young man pushed from behind, and they managed after a good deal of exertion and several recuperative pauses to reach the top, find her bedroom, and shut her inside. As they stood on the landing, struggling to recover their breath, Waithe felt as though they had successfully smuggled a corpse into the house under the very noses of a cordon of invisible police, and he was tempted to congratulate the young man on his part in what to him must have seemed an almost ghoulish enterprise. But just then the bedroom door softly opened, a slim white hand reached out of the darkness for the young man, and Dorothy's voice murmured something indistinguishable about that *bayooteevil antrooodeeng beeg toe*. The young man reacted as if he had been sharing Waithe's thoughts. Upon feeling himself clutched and on the point of being drawn, as it were, by some unseen force of lecherous witchcraft into the room, he stood for a single horrified second like a small boy confronting a ghost in a cemetery, then let out a frightened yelp, jerked free, and went pounding off at great speed down the stairs. Waithe took hold of the hand, which was now groping eagerly around in space, and gently maneuvered it back into the room and closed the door. He waited for a while on the landing until the confused muttering inside the room gave way at last to regular breathing and finally to small discordant wheezes and snores. Then he went down the stairs and out the door to his car.

As he drove home through the gradually graying darkness, Waithe pondered the curious dreamlike character which the events of the evening—indeed, of the whole period since Dorothy's arrival to lecture—had taken on in his mind. It was not merely that they reminded him—as events so often did in Cranton—of something he felt he recalled having read long ago in a novel. It was more that they seemed part of a bad novel which, perhaps equally long ago, he himself had written, a novel in which, for reasons that had eluded him at the time, he had somehow failed to engage the reality of the heroine, and so had created a ghost. The trouble with Dorothy as heroine was that she was always on the verge of disappearing into the dusty grab bag of her type—that whole scrappy complex of cliché and patched-up histrionic clothing for which, whether in novels or in life, Waithe had a deep, almost paranoid contempt. Just at the moment when one felt on the point of being able at last to *see* her as she personally was, she would squirm maddeningly out from under one's vision and proceed to transform herself into something so commonly and tritely seen by so many others that she could no longer be seen at all by anyone with taste. She kept giving up the individuality which she must innately have possessed to this tattered, shopworn ghost concocted out of other people's shopworn seeing. Her own unique humanity kept fading out like her voice in the heavy interference set up by all that faulty perception, and one had constantly to tune her in again, but with a touch far more certain and sensitive than Waithe knew his own to be.

Part, he realized, of his ambivalent vision of her—or his ambivalent lack of vision—stemmed from the unreality of the past which they had so long ago shared together. It was exactly as unreal to him now as Shelby's past with Buchanan, and for most of the same reasons: it, too, was a cliché and—what was far worse—it had, at least in its broad outlines, long since been written out in that massive collection of equally massive novels which had come to represent, and had very largely replaced, in his mind the experience he had had with Dorothy during the war. He could no longer envision the experience now except in the way the novels said it had occurred, and whenever he did so, he was always brought up jarringly short against some G.I. wet-dream fantasy of a woman, a sort of foxhole–slit trench succubus, who, while she was nothing at all like Dorothy as she had actually been, was very like Dorothy as, in both fantasy and life, she appeared to have become. Besides, that past seemed, each time he thought of it, to demand from him some form of recognition or assent; it insisted upon being taken in hand and dealt with, brought up to date and renewed, like a loan note that was long overdue at the bank, or a deathbed charge passed down to him by a murdered ancestor to avenge the family honor. Yet this was just what he felt, particularly in the light of recent events, least capable of doing. Not only had he lost his hold on the reality of that past and seen it fictionalized out of existence besides, but he could see no connection between Dorothy then and Dorothy now. It was as if in killing the past, he had killed her, too, and her resurrection here in Cranton had indeed been like the return of a ghost to haunt him for the crime. But the whole, perhaps terrible point was that it had not haunted him. It had only given him the awkward feeling of having to be nice to someone who looked vaguely familiar and was therefore deserving of courtesy until the question of whether they actually knew each other could be cleared up. In order to have done anything more, he would have had to have reduced himself back, through a gigantic act of will and memory, to that canceled-out earlier time, re-created it in his mind exactly as it was, and he could no more have done that with the Dorothy he now knew there before him than he could have restored Buchanan to his pristine Edenic condition, or put back the swamps on which Cranton now stood. Present reality in the case of all of them was much too vigorously present; it had the inestimable advantage of being quite unavoidably *there*; and they were trapped in it, stranded upon it, exhausted and gasping, where the ceaseless tides of time and history had happened to cast them up.

Still, Waithe could not resist wondering whether beneath all the reasons he gave himself for his helplessness, his inability to engage things as they were, there might not be some deeply buried, ultimately contradictory reason which he had not yet found the nerve to face. It came to him that there might be some other way of giving assent, of acknowledging the existence of Dorothy, Buchanan, Cranton, and even of himself in spite of the irrevocable pastness of the past and its obliterated connection with the present. And as he thought back over the dreamlike events of the evening, he asked himself whether, if he had been equipped with a knowledge of that other way, he might have responded to the hand that Dorothy had reached out of the darkness and have allowed *himself* to be drawn into the room. It was possible that, had he done so, he might have found her passion irresistible and have answered it with a passion of his own that he had not then felt, and in that passion have discovered himself and her alive and feeling at last in the inescapably real, no longer dreamlike present. But even as he let the thought form in his mind, he knew that it, too, was fantasy, the easy way out so tantalizingly proffered by fatigue, sentimentality, and pre-dawn hangover. It was exactly what, in the interests of the tight hold he had upon the irreducible reality of fact, he could least afford, particularly at this time, to permit himself. So it was that upon turning in at his driveway he was overcome by an immense urge to go to sleep and sink once again into that mindless oblivion, the natural abode of fantasy, in which all things, while patently unreal, can be recognized and dismissed as such with the recovery of the self, in its own time and on its own terms, to the wary life of consciousness.

CHAPTER VI

1.

At the party commemorating the end of
Dorothy's lectures, Buchanan's second gigantic howl of the
evening—inspired a moment before by Anthony Marsh's lin-
gually impotent attempt at brilliance—had died dismally away
in the room. The young wives had ceased to shriek and throw
themselves hysterically about like a gaggle of harpies in heat,
and Marsh himself, still conscious of being skewered on the
point of Buchanan's soul-puncturing stare, was making a manly
effort to renew the pretense of sincerity behind his forced
political laugh. Waithe was briefly moved to feel sorry for him,
but since he had just had a demonstration of the young man's
singular talent for turning even humiliation to social advantage, he decided to bestow his sympathy instead upon someone whose talent worked in the exact opposite manner and
turned every social advantage into humiliation. Dorothy, on
whom his eye now came to rest, was sitting as he had first seen
her that evening—leaning far back on the sofa, displaying her
very remarkable knees, and looking out over the rim of her
freshly refilled cocktail glass. But he noticed at once that her
expression had changed, and that her face, which before had
been relaxed and rather dreamily speculative, was now drawn

141

into a tight grimace of concentration. Her idle study of the room had at some point given way to a fixed and seemingly obsessive examination of the one corner of it which Buchanan, Marsh, and the young wives had for some time occupied. She was quite simply staring at them—or perhaps only at Buchanan—as if her life depended on what, by staring hard enough, she might be able to see, as if by staring she might in the end embarrass whatever or whoever it was into yielding up a shameful secret or blurting out a guilty confession that would exonerate her of some charge—although whether she stared in fascination or contempt Waithe could not begin to imagine. It came over him, however, that her concentration could very well have been set off by the sound of Buchanan's first howl, that she had, like everyone except himself, been shocked by it, but for reasons that turned on the fact that, unlike everyone except again himself, she *had* heard it before, reasons that were hidden away in the whole dark mystery of the happenings of that night when she had first heard it. If that was the case, the howl had apparently called up in her emotions relating to Buchanan which explained and perhaps even justified her staring at him; hence, it was with the excited feeling of being at last on the track of a clue to that perplexing mystery that Waithe watched her. As he did so, he noticed that she was being watched by others, too. The three sociologists whose names Waithe could never remember had suspended their conspiratorial whisperings over by the piano and were now studying her with mild scientific eyes as though they also felt, and obscurely hoped, that she was about to do something, perhaps in their case something such as she would have done had she been a character in a Hornblower or Fleischmann novel. But she disappointed them, as in a different respect she disappointed Waithe. She did not gulp down her cocktail, rise from the sofa, wobble, and slowly begin taking off her clothes, nor did she do any of the things which might have reassured Waithe that he was not simply following a false lead in his speculations about her emotional state and the reasons behind it. She only sat there, sipping her drink, and kept her eyes on Buchanan's corner as if looking to him, as they were looking to her, for something indescribable or ultimately revelatory to happen.

2.

In the next moment Waithe's observations were interrupted by an acute visceral sense of imminent peril, and he looked away from Dorothy in time to see himself being borne down upon by one of the young wives whom he knew only by the inappropriately poetic name of Sylvia. She had shortly before been a part of the worshipful throng surrounding Buchanan, but evidently she had grown restless in so passive a role and had gone browsing among the assembled guests in search of someone to test her surgical instruments on. She had picked Waithe—as he well knew—because she had never quite been able to figure him out and lived in hope of one day being able to capture and pickle him for her collection. Almost everyone else she had sooner or later managed to classify and pin down for dissection on the little laboratory table which she kept set up in some antiseptic corner of her paranoia. But about him she was still irritatedly uncertain. His phylum, genus, species, or whatever it was continued to elude her, and she clearly experienced great anxiety whenever she was around him because she seemed unable to make up her mind whether he was something genuinely new in the biological world or something so tritely old that she had never bothered to read up on his type. In any event, he intrigued her, and she came at him now as though she were going to knock him down and pop him into a bottle just to relieve her indecision. Upon seeing her approach, Waithe instinctively drew back a step, and then in a feeble effort to justify the movement, he cringed and threw his arms up over his head in a mock gesture of self-defense. But Sylvia had no humor, only choler. She planted herself solidly before him, brought her parched, death's-head face with its unblinking, mad blue eyes and perpetual morgue attendant's smile close against his own unadorned one, and began to peer into him as though she expected him at any moment to start partitioning himself in some interesting new mitotic way. The expression on her face, which was exactly like the expression he had once seen on the face of a man who had been fished out of Cranton River after floating for three weeks in the hot summer sun, reminded Waithe of the time he had come upon her standing in the stacks of the University Library. She had been clutching the latest issue of Buchanan's review and staring raptly at the cover, on which, as he had already noticed, there appeared in the tiniest of print her name and the title of a poem she had somehow persuaded Buchanan to publish. Waithe had watched her for several long minutes while she stood there goggling and twitching, her body strained forward in an agony of self-adulation. Then, fearing that she might any second scream out and fall frothing to the floor, he had gone up to her and inquired politely if she was having an orgasm. She had taken no notice of him whatever, at least no conscious notice. Her eyes had moved slowly up from the magazine and focused for an instant on some invisible point on the opposite wall, and her chapped lips had curled a little higher over her long, sharp, yellow teeth. But then almost at once she had stared down again, and her tongue had licked lasciviously out and up over the peeling skin of her lips.

She looked like that now—it even occurred to Waithe that perhaps she *always* looked like that—and he wondered if, in spite of her regular field trips into the tangled interiors of other people's psyches, she ever took conscious notice of anyone. It was, therefore, with the idea of trying to establish some sort of liaison with her, at a level on which she would be fairly certain to respond, that he started to ask her if she had been publishing any good poems lately. But he only just managed to get his mouth open when she grasped him by the arm and began to shake him convulsively as she launched into a shrill harangue about status in Cranton. It seemed she had evolved a theory—or at least a culture of one—in some damp germ-garden of her brain that people who had genuine status in Cranton never made the first move in social situations, but were always *approached* by others. As she developed this argument, she kept glaring wildly about the room as if canvassing for examples, all the while tightening her grip on Waithe's arm and shaking him like a child trying to filch pennies out of a piggy bank. In an effort to extricate himself without antagonizing her, Waithe summoned the nerve to confess that he had never actually noticed this, but that it certainly was an interesting idea and very probably a true one, and that he had often wondered himself just how you *could* tell exactly who had status in Cranton. As he said this, he realized that his voice carried about as much conviction as that of a male nurse humoring a patient in the violent ward at Bellevue. But then he saw that it made no difference whatever, since Sylvia was obviously not listening to a word he said. Her hand had fallen from his arm, and she was looking steadily over his shoulder, her eyes wide and gleaming with some fanatical inner light as though she had just caught a glimpse of the Blessed Trinity. *You see,* she hissed, flickering her tongue excitedly up over her grainy lips. *HE has status. They approach HIM.* Waithe turned just as a small procession of people, led by a young woman carrying a homemade paper crown on a pillow, came filing across the room and stopped before the chair in which Buchanan was sitting. With an air of great ceremony the young woman went around behind Buchanan, deposited the pillow on a table, lifted the crown high, and slowly lowered it onto his head, saying, as she did so, *I hereby proclaim thee King Arthur Buchanan, last of the illustrious house of Bourbon and Hangover, lord of the imperial quart, emperor of royal highness, and supreme spirit-ual ruler of Cranton, its territories and dominions.* She then placed scepter-wise in his hand a large bottle of bourbon which had been passed to her, and the whole group began to sing "Happy birthday to you." In a moment almost everyone in the room had joined in the singing; the hostess appeared carrying a white cake on which a solitary enormous candle burned; and there followed a great many cries of congratulations and best wishes, while Buchanan beamed beatifically from his corner and drew the sign of the cross several times in the air. Sylvia stood entranced through this performance, her eyes glittering wetly with excitement and her lips drawn back in a smile suggestive of a depraved Mona Lisa undergoing a high colonic. Then she moved dreamily off toward Buchanan as though impelled by an irresistible impulse to go over and kiss the hem of his garment. Waithe, to whom the realization that the party was being held in Buchanan's as well as Dorothy's honor had come as a distinct but meaningless surprise, took the opportunity afforded him by Sylvia's departure to escape into the crowd. Then, feeling suddenly in need of a drink, he made his way toward the kitchen where the liquor was kept.

3.

As he went through the swinging door into the kitchen, he very nearly collided with Miriam Hornblower and Lester Fleischmann who were standing by the liquor table passionately engaged in kissing each other. Upon seeing him they quickly drew apart; Miriam turned on her ghastly grin; Lester ran a nervous hand through his crew cut; and they began talking as though they had been interrupted in the middle of a deeply earnest conversation. Waithe mumbled something inconsequential and proceeded to make himself a drink, feeling as he did so as if he had blundered into the penultimately scandalous chapter of a novel one of them might have been writing. It was not merely that this was just the sort of incident they would have included in a novel, but that the circumstances behind it—particularly if they had involved anyone except themselves—were exactly the kind they would have taken the most gleeful delight in riddling to shreds with those deadly automatic weapons they used instead of typewriters. For Waithe happened to know that the seemingly tender embrace he had interrupted was actually just another strategic maneuver in Lester's carefully calculated campaign to win dominance over Miriam by getting at her emotionally and perhaps in the end—if he had his usual luck—sexually.

The trouble was that Lester and Miriam were too much

alike to be able to inhabit the same world without the bitterest of rivalry. They were, in fact, so very much alike—even to the extent of knowing all the same people and sharing the same opinions about them—that it was almost impossible to tell their books apart, and reviewers were always infuriating them by solemnly comparing a new work of one with the previous achievement of the other. Together they constituted— albeit with ferocious unwillingness—a sort of bicephalous Louella Parsons of the intellectual life, but exactly which was Louella and which Parsons was a question to which, considering the close similarity of their thoughts and works, no one took much time or trouble seeking an answer. It was enough, particularly for those of their ex-friends who regularly, with almost every new publishing season, saw themselves and their loved ones massacred in print, that they were both fearsomely accomplished novelists of other people's manners, good or bad, and had about as much respect for personal privacy as a pair of obstetrical interns doing ward research on the malformations of the uterus. Anthony Marsh, however, who had once sat for a particularly vicious portrait of a Guggenheim Fellowship bum in a Fleischmann novel, had retaliated by suggesting on one occasion that Lester was really a sort of *female* Miriam Hornblower, and that had since been generally accepted as the nicest distinction it was possible to make between them. The fact was that Miriam, for all her softly obtrusive neckdown femininity, was as mentally male behind her refrigerated cadaver's grin as a woman could be and still be allowed to use the ladies' washroom. One was never quite sure in her presence whether to offer her a seat or a cigar, but it was very likely, since she was onto such tactics, that she would have played it straight and taken both. Lester, on the other hand, had the mind of a psychopathic Ivy League co-ed, and the face of her tennis-playing twin brother at Yale. One saw his type regularly, gazing blandly out of newspaper photographs of just apprehended ax murderers, child molesters, and compulsive arsonists: the big, round, innocent, blue eyes that came to life only when a crowded tenement was in flames; the clean, pink, baby-boy features that always looked relaxed even when the little girl protested that she didn't want to take a nice long ride in the big shiny car. The only trouble with Lester was that his feminine streak caused him to depend too much on his face to get him out of difficulties which his mind goaded him into creating. He never seemed able to believe that with his looks anyone could possibly think badly of him; therefore, he never bothered to conceal his crimes behind the crafty dissimulations which Miriam, with her earthier masculine shrewdness, had learned to employ. Everything with him was open and aboveboard; he had nothing to hide but his treachery; and he had long ago decided that that *was* hidden. Whatever he thought, he said; whatever he did, he wrote about. If he had an affair, he made it into a short story, taking care to see that the person involved could be clearly recognized and divorce action taken. On one historic occasion he had wrecked the marriage of a former college roommate by sleeping with his wife, and then publishing the intimate details in a national magazine, and sending his old friend a complimentary copy with the appropriate passages outlined in red. It was not so much that he wanted to do positive harm to anyone, although he quite evidently did. It was just that he could never imagine a person with a face like his doing any harm.

In Miriam, however, he seemed to have met someone who threatened not only to equal him professionally but to find him out psychologically, and since his superiority in the one respect was essential to his invulnerability in the other, he was clearly in a position calling for desperate measures. But the difficulty was that none of his standard measures seemed likely, in Miriam's case, to prove desperate enough, and there were no others he could imagine resorting to without taking the risk of being thought badly of, or—what was far worse— thinking badly of himself. Miriam was much too clever and too practiced to allow herself to be disarmed by any of the ordinary forms of literary blackmail and duress; it would have been like trying to throw a half nelson on Nelson. If he had written about her, she would simply have grinned and written about him, and he had a fairly strong conviction that, in a contest of that kind, he would wind up with his shoulders on the canvas. For while he had not yet found her out, he was very much afraid that, given any provocation, she shortly would him, or at least make it brilliantly appear that she had, which in the end would come down to the same deplorable thing. In the face of this impasse he began for the first time in his life to feel consciously on the verge of really wanting to do someone positive harm, and the sheer frightfulness of the impulse so shocked him that he at once gave over his self-esteem to the protective custody of the one idea not involving homicide that seemed likely to promise a solution to his problem. He evidently decided that the thing to do to get rid of Miriam in the competitive running as well as neutralize her inclination to find him out was to make her fall in love with him. After that it would be a simple matter to persuade himself that he in turn had fallen in love with her, thereby restoring his self-esteem—if only on a short-term probation—to its rightful place. If he could succeed in doing this, he would be doing the one thing which he could imagine and excuse a person with his face doing. He would, in fact, be using his face to save it, just as he would, with luck, be using his maleness to arouse the woman in Miriam's body and at the same time to cuckold the male in her mind. It was to that end, therefore, that in all simplicity and good faith he had for some time been directing his best energies.

4.

Waithe had, quite by accident, blundered upon the scene of Lester's endeavors—as well as upon such evidence as he had for his theories about Lester's motives—one night after a party several months previously. Lester and Miriam had devoted the bulk of the evening to their usual party pastime of conversationally out-hating each other. Yet Waithe had noticed even then that Lester's performance was not up to its normally high standard of nastiness, and that he had lost more than one round to Miriam as a result evidently of some defect of concentration which his steady intake of scotches had done nothing to correct. Later on after the party ended he had insisted even more inexplicably, in what in anyone else could easily have been taken for a gesture of drunken courtliness, upon gathering together some people and driving to the station to see Miriam off on her train back to New York. Waithe, Anthony Marsh, and a young female archaeologist named Alice had rather dubiously agreed to go along. They had all piled into the back of Lester's ranch wagon, and Lester had driven off with such a sudden burst of speed that Alice, who was not yet seated, had been thrown violently against Waithe—a position which she at once secured by half sitting, half lying down in his lap and clutching him frantically around the neck as the car sped and swerved through the mercifully deserted streets. At the station they found that, because of Lester's haste, they had several minutes to wait for the train, and while the others were preoccupied with urgent interior speculations on the unlikelihood of their being still alive, Lester and Miriam walked a short distance down the platform. For some time no one spoke, and there was no sound except the thin scraping of some leaves that blew with apparent purposefulness along the tracks. But then something like a gasp came from Anthony Marsh, and Waithe looked around just as Lester and Miriam moved together in the shadows and fell into a deep and seemingly passionate embrace. They stood there clasped in each other's arms for several seconds, while the others began making badly co-ordinated attempts at conversation and tried and failed to keep from staring. Then they changed their base of operations to a bench and settled down to some serious necking, in the course of which Lester appeared to have pawed open the front of Miriam's blouse and to be engaged in kissing the nipples of her breasts. Waithe decided at this point that it was time he proposed to the others that they all move down to the other end of the platform, but just as he started to do so, Miriam threw back her head and let out one of her high-pitched, derisive laughs. This was immediately followed by some sort of exclamation from Lester, and a moment later by the foghorn bellow from up the tracks of the approaching train. Then Miriam was standing up and fumbling hurriedly at the front of her blouse; the train came hissing and steaming into the station; Miriam walked forward and climbed aboard; and Waithe and the others caught a glimpse of her grinning face and upraised hand as the train moved slowly past them, gathered speed, and slid away into the darkness.

On thinking back over the events of that night—with all that he later came to intuit concerning Lester's motives— Waithe was at a loss to account for what happened next. Several explanations were possible, and the validity of each depended on how one saw Lester or, perhaps more correctly, on which Lester one saw. It might well have been Miriam's laugh that touched the whole thing off, for coming as it did at the very apex of his strenuous amatory display, it could easily have shocked Lester into the awful realization that, far from having taken Miriam in, he may actually have allowed her to find him out. In that case, he had, in all hypocritical good conscience, sped her fondly on her way to New York with just the evidence she needed to blackmail him for the rest of his life. It was also perfectly possible, considering how drunk he was and how hard it must have been for him, even while drunk, to pretend to make love to a woman he despised, that his internal defenses had simply collapsed under the strain, and that, for a few terrible seconds, the repressed psychopath in him had gone raging out of control and burst through the placid, baby-blue-eyed façade. It was even possible—although scarcely reconcilable with the Lester that Waithe knew—that in some weird moment of maudlin weakness he had actually caught himself entertaining the appalling idea that he really was in love with Miriam and had honestly *felt* all the passion which he had been so smugly sure he was faking, and which, in the last extremity, he had only planned to *pretend* to his conscience was sincere. In that case, the unspeakable irony of his position could easily have been too much for his fuddled mind and have accounted for the violence of his subsequent behavior.

But whatever the reason—and it might have been any one or any combination of these—the fact was that Lester, a moment after Miriam's departure, had gone suddenly and devastatingly berserk.

Waithe's first knowledge of this singular occurrence came in the form of a nightmarish vision of Lester charging madly up the station platform, emitting as he ran peculiar hydrophobic cries and roars and flailing his arms violently about as though defending himself against a swarm of attacking bees. Waithe initially supposed that he was simply giving vent to a certain animal excitement which had been aroused but not fully relieved by his session with Miriam. But then as Lester came abreast of him and kept on going, and he had a glimpse of his popping eyes and contorted face, Waithe realized that something far more serious was the matter. He turned then and shouted to Anthony Marsh and Alice, who were standing a little way off in what appeared to be a state of profound shock, and they all began running frantically about as though the bees which seemed to have been pursuing Lester had suddenly caught up with them. Lester had by that time reached the door of the deserted waiting room and burst inside, and when at last the others had regained their senses and hurried in after him, they found him standing in the middle of the room holding a large metal waste container high over his head. For a moment he held it there as though uncertain what to do with it. Then he twirled it wrestler-fashion, threw it with a tremendous crash to the floor, and began jumping up and down on it. After he had thoroughly mashed in one side of it and squashed a great quantity of paper out onto the floor, he picked the container up, carried it out on the platform, and hurled it with another tremendous crash down onto the train tracks. He then came back inside, puffing and blowing and histrionically dusting his hands, and proceeded to rip all the bars off the closed ticket window. The bars came off as though they had been stuck on with scotch tape, and the others were so awed by his violence and strength that no one made a move to stop him. After he had pulled all the bars off, he carefully gathered them up, and cradling them like a sheaf of spears in one arm, threw them one by one through each of the several windows that faced the street. When the sound of shattering glass had died away, he stood for some seconds glaring balefully around the room and convulsively clenching and unclenching his fists. Then he caught sight of the illuminated cigarette machine standing in one corner, lurched over to it, raised his foot, and kicked in the front of it, sending a spray of cigarette packages and glass fragments flying all over the floor. At this point Waithe, who had been praying steadily for the imminent arrival of the police, summoned the nerve to go up to him and take hold of his arm. Lester stared blankly at him and then down at the hand on his arm, slowly blew out his breath in a long, quavering sigh, and went bounding off through the door and into the street. He ran up the sidewalk to his ranch wagon, flung himself in behind the wheel, and the others, not knowing what else to do, followed along and climbed in after him.

Lester drove off with a gravel-grinding lunge that threw Alice once again violently into Waithe, and by the time they had recovered their balance, the car was doing at least seventy, and Lester was making no allowance whatever for curves. In the curiously shuddering glow of the headlights Waithe could just see over the back of the front seat the gray, frightened blob of Anthony Marsh's face and, next to it, the dark outlines of Lester's close-cropped head and fiercely hunched shoulders. Above the high whine of the engine he could hear Alice sniveling in a series of queer broken gasps that were like the sound of a pneumonia patient fighting for breath. Then they would go squealing into a curve; Alice would moan; and Waithe would involuntarily shut his eyes as the teetering outward swing of the car pressed him heavily against her, and her fingernails dug deep into his knee. Then the car would reluctantly right itself, almost as though it were already resigned to the ditch, and they would go rocketing on into the night, as trapped as monkeys in outer space. They drove in this fashion for what seemed like hours, with Lester taking the curves literally on two wheels and the car weaving and pitching drunkenly all over the road. Then suddenly as they entered the outskirts of Cranton something inside Lester seemed slowly to begin running down. The car gradually slackened speed; Lester's shoulders ever so slightly sagged; and by the time they reached the center of town, they were moving along at a sedate thirty-five; and Lester was proposing—quite as if they were just driving back from a pleasant day in the country—that they all come up to his place for a nightcap. For a moment or two no one said anything, for it was impossible to tell what Lester might do if crossed. But finally Waithe, who had long since passed far beyond courage and fear and was now feeling nothing whatever, declined the invitation for all of them and asked that they be let out at the next corner. Lester at once obliged by violently wrenching the wheel, driving up onto the sidewalk, and coming to an instantaneous, bouncy stop not three feet in front of a large tree. Waithe and the others got out and stood numbly at the curb while Lester backed with a great scraping and roaring into the street, gave them one of his clean-cut Ivy League smiles and a cheerful wave, and went racing off into the darkness.

As he stood there watching the car's taillights disappear up the street, Waithe became aware of the abrupt return of feeling to his body. It was as though he had just come down off a high mountain and his arteries had suddenly filled up with blood and popped like ears. But it was not until he was undressing for bed in the first pale hour of dawn that he recovered himself sufficiently to feel the smarting pain in his knee and to notice the tiny puncture marks where Alice's nails had dug deep into his skin. They remained there slightly infected and unhealed for some time as a sort of stubbornly insistent memento of the night's experiences. But as it turned out, they were about all that remained. Everything else seemed to have been swept under some rug or dropped down an Orwellian memory hole or carted away after nightfall to whatever dump heap it was where Cranton discreetly disposed of its unwanted experiences. Everything else had been scrupulously deleted from the account books of time and history, and no one ever spoke of any of it again. All that was left was the single tantalizing scrap of perhaps illusory evidence which now confronted Waithe as he stood in the kitchen mixing his drink, and which seemed to challenge him to make as much or as little of it as he would—the sight of Lester still earnestly, and with every appearance of good faith, making his play, while Miriam looked innocently into his eyes and grinned, her face showing no expression of any kind except just possibly the faintest hint of contempt.

5.

Upon returning to the living room, Waithe was not surprised to see that very little appeared to have changed during his brief absence. The air of tension which shortly before he had felt—or imagined he had felt—in the room seemed to have been dissipated in the merriment that had followed Buchanan's coronation, and all the people looked as though they had relaxed back into their normal condition of stasis, in which state they gave the effect of frieze figures graven on the sides of a Grecian urn—the huntsman perpetually drawing back his spear to bring down the forever fleeing hind, the lover perpetually reaching out for his beloved who forever dances just beyond his outstretched arms. But there were no huntsmen visible among the assembled guests and, so far as Waithe could tell, no lovers. Buchanan, his paper crown now slightly askew, still sat enthroned in his corner surrounded by his bedazzled retinue, although now Anthony Marsh was seated intimately at his right hand and looking—if one could judge by the light of incipient salvation in his eyes—very much as if he might be about to finagle that fellowship after all. Dorothy still occupied her solitary seat of vigil over on the sofa, still held Buchanan under her somberly intent, spiritually X-raying, ever so slightly glazed scrutiny. The three sociologists next to the piano continued to observe her, only now with the help of a fresh round of drinks their interest appeared to have grown less scientific and more frankly anatomical, for one of them was leaning close to the other two and cupping his hand significantly up to his breast, and they were all laughing rather openly in her direction and at her expense. The only really complete change in the room was the presence at the piano of

158

the genial host of the evening, the chairman of the Classics Department which had sponsored Dorothy's lectures. He had just finished a particularly villainous imitation of Tom Lehrer singing "Be Prepared" and was now progressing into the opening strains of "My Home Town"—the chorus of which he customarily revised so that the words "my home town" became "my old Cranton." At the moment he was leaning far back on the piano stool, pounding hard on the keys, and braying at the top of his voice—his head and shoulders weaving vigorously about in an evident transport of bibulous delight.

Just then with the abruptness of a pistol shot there rang out through the room above the noise he was making the single shouted name **BUCHANAN!** For an eternity of a moment nothing whatever happened. The host went on with his song; the assembled guests went on with their conversations; somewhere in the world a dog undoubtedly went on with the pursuit of his doggy life. Then the shouted name rang out again, and this time everything stopped like an old movie in mid-reel. People appeared to be transfixed with their legs suspended in air, their glasses halfway to their lips. The host sat like Harold Lloyd gaping into a broken-down film projector, his hands splayed out six inches above the keyboard and his mouth wide open. There was a silence so excruciatingly painful that it could not have been improved upon if someone had been caught defecating on the floor of Buckingham Palace in full view of the royal family. Heartbeats seemed to stop, the flow of life to cease. An emergency squad bursting through the door just then would have taken one look around and pronounced the whole crowd officially dead. Then everyone turned at once and saw Dorothy standing in the middle of the room, wobbling slightly, her cocktail glass tipped steeply in one hand, her face twisted into a fantastic Halloween mask of outrage—looking for all the world as though she had just stepped out of some madly drunken party scene in a Hornblower or Fleischmann novel. Waithe half expected her to complete the travesty and start taking off her clothes, and the three sociologists looked as though they passionately hoped she would. But she just stood there and glared at Buchanan as if debating whether to rush over and claw him to bits. Then she drew herself up, propped one hand shrewishly on her hip, lifted her dripping glass to eye level, and squinted meanly over the rim at him. She even bent forward, still holding the glass to her eye, and waveringly affected to inspect him dowager-like from head to toe. Then suddenly, in one quick movement, she straightened, threw back her head, gulped down the drink, took a somewhat shuddery breath, and began to speak. The words came rocketing out of her as though she had been stock-piling them for a thousand years, and almost before their sense had had time to penetrate Waithe's consciousness, he became aware of the singular fact that they were being spoken without any trace of accent whatsoever. Somehow at an obscure moment in the course of the evening Dorothy had been at least verbally transformed— either that or she had for some reason abruptly ceased to pretend to be something she was not, had by necessity or choice given up the bewildering, perhaps intentionally absurd disguise with which her accent had for so long provided her. And as he contemplated that fact and tried at the same time to listen to what she was saying, Waithe realized that such a thing could have come about only through some profoundly inner, even disastrously inner crisis of conversion, the explosive effects of which he and the others were now uncomfortably on the point of witnessing.

As he realized this, Waithe also had an acute premonition that the truth—for it could only be that—of the relationship between Dorothy and Buchanan was at long last coming out into the open, and he concluded that his first intuition was about to be proven correct, that Dorothy had in fact, on that mysterious evening many weeks before, been the victim of a drunken rape, and was now confronting her attacker like the proverbial wronged maiden of Victorian fiction, in the way best calculated to harm him most—on the very scene and before the very sponsors of his stanchest claim to honor and virtue. Yet her choice of this particular time and place was obviously more than a brilliant piece of strategy, although just what more it was Waithe could not begin to guess. It was, in fact, on the basis of the evidence at hand, inconceivable that she should be confronting him at all, at this or any time or place, and that the experience, however humiliating it may have been, should even especially have affected her. For Dorothy, after all, was no maiden, and rather than being adversely affected by humiliation, she positively reveled in it, particularly when she was being raped. It was inconceivable *unless* something had just lately struck her so forcibly that it had catalyzed some buried hostility to Buchanan—more deeply buried even than her taste for humiliation—into an uncontrollable need then and there for revenge. As to the nature of that something Waithe already had his suspicions, since he had noticed earlier in the evening what he took to be her shocked reaction to Buchanan's howl. Furthermore, what she now seemed to be saying confirmed his suspicions, for the issue of the howl was uppermost in it, was, it appeared, her principal—although, if he was right, only her ostensibly principal—ground of complaint. The *significance* of the howl in her mind was, he knew, the important thing, and it was with the hope of at last determining what that significance was that he tried now to listen both to her words and to the tenuous vibrations of meaning behind them.

Buchanan, she was saying in a mock-serious tone of persuasion, *it would please me ever so much to hear you howl like that again. It brings back such* Tender Memories, *Buchanan. It fills me with such exCruciating* Emotion. *You'll do it again for me, won't you, Buchanan? Just once more, just for me. A nice* Big *one just for me. Come* On, *Buchanan, Howl for me, just for* Me. *You know something, everybody?* He *has a howl for every* Occasion, *for every* Single, Solitary Occasion. Can *you imagine* That? *He even has a special one for me, just for* Me, *for my very, very own. Come on, Buchanan, tell them about how you howled just for me once. Come on, you remember. Show all these nice people how you did it. A nice* Big *one. Come* On Now, *you remember.* Ahhwoooooo, *it went just like a great big* Ferocious *lion. Nice and* Louud *and sudden just like a lion. It positively gave me* Goose Pimples, *didn't it, Buchanan? I even screamed, it was so loud and sudden. But* You *didn't care. You* didn't care the least Lil Bit. *You were so* Ferocious *and* Masterful *you didn't care about anything, did you? No, you* Didn't. *Not one* Snap. *Not one* Dir-ty Lil Snap.

As she said this, she moved unsteadily up to him and snapped her fingers in his face, then stepped back and stood staring defiantly down at him. But Buchanan did not stir; he never even blinked. He just sat there and stared back at her with no expression whatever in his eyes. On the chair beside him Anthony Marsh had turned the color of dirty wash, and on the faces of the young wives scattered on the floor at his feet anxiety began breaking out like some species of instantaneous acne. But Buchanan just sat there, horribly and relentlessly immobile, as though nothing in him had ever felt or lived. Upon sensing his resistance Dorothy went up to him again and this time shoved his paper crown down hard on his head, so hard that it almost slid over his eyes. But he still made no move, spoke no word, gave no sign, and in the whole room life once again seemed to pause without even a caught breath, as if waiting for someone to die. In the awful silence Dorothy suddenly seemed for the first time to feel herself alone. She stood there in front of Buchanan, looking bewildered and panicky and on the verge of tears, like a child who had forgotten her lines in the middle of a recitation. Then she recovered herself, glared contemptuously down at Buchanan, and said, *What's the* Matter, *Buchanan? Can't you get it up?* When he still said nothing, did nothing, an expression almost of pity came into her face, and she murmured, *No, you can't. You really, really can't.* Then suddenly, as if a wonderful idea had just struck her, she turned excitedly to the silent assemblage of guests and, her eyes murderously bright, said, *You want to know something, people? You want to know the* Real, Real Truth? *Well, he* Really Can't *get it up. He can't get it up* At All. *Not* One . . . Lil . . . Inch. *Not one* Sin-gle Sol-itary Inch. *He's all a* Lie *and a* Cheat. *Buchanan,* she said, turning back to face him, *you're nothing but a* Lie *and a* Cheat. *Furthermore, you are a* Fake, *a* Phony, *a* Liar, *and a* Queer. *All you ever do is* Talk, *just* Talk. *But you never* Do *anything. Why don't you ever write poems any more? I hear you were a good* Poet *once, Buchanan. But not any* More. *You're a* Failed *poet now, a real failed* Has-Been *poet. You can't get it up* There *any more*

163

either, can you? It won't Come *any more there either, will it? But that isn't the* Only *secret I know about you, is it, Buchanan? Shall I tell them the* Real Big Juicy One? *Do you want me to* Tell *them, Buchanan? Shall I announce to the world what I* Really *know about you? Well, I'll just tell you, especially* You, she said, indicating the little cluster of young wives at Buchanan's feet. You'll *be simply* Amazed. *Well, the truth is that he really hates and despises women and likes to hurt them, don't you, Buchanan? That's how he gets his kicks. That's what makes him howl. He can't get it up any more, so he takes it out on* Women. *He would have been quite a* Man *with a bull whip at Dachau. But of course you don't believe it, do you?* You just couldn't *Possibly believe an awful thing like that about your big beautiful* Genius *in the funny paper* Hat. *It just doesn't seem* Possible, *does it?* All right. *I'll* Show you. *I've got* Evidence. Real *evidence.* And with that she ripped the front of her dress savagely open, pulled out one of her large breasts, and aimed it straight at Buchanan, as though she were about to shoot him down on the spot. The nipple looked swollen and blue and oddly mangled, as if it had been nipped with a pair of pliers or punched by a mailed fist. *He did that,* she screamed in crazy triumph. *He got me* Drunk *and did* That. *And then he* Howled, *the* Son-of-a-Bitch. *He* Howled. Then she lifted the breast higher and stood looking sadly and wonderingly down at it, lost for that one brief moment to Buchanan, the people in the room, and all the fury she had loosed upon them, in tender contemplation of the miracle that this poor, hurt, defenseless thing actually belonged to her.

It came over Waithe then—almost with the sensation that it was happening inside his own body—that the rasping knife of irony had at last been given its final twist. For now the life of Cranton appeared in fact to have risen or descended to that level of supreme grotesqueness at which it was indistinguishable from the image of life to be found in the typical Hornblower or Fleischmann novel. Dorothy had indeed gulped down her drink, wobbled, and begun taking off her clothes. Nature had indeed begun to imitate art. Or had *their* art been imitating *this* nature all along, and he had just never been aware of it until now? Waithe had no way of knowing, had literally no way of knowing anything other than what he knew, and because he did not, it suddenly seemed to him terribly important to take stock of what now he *did* know—as if by taking stock he might still be able to salvage a little confidence in his apparently highly fallible powers of understanding. What he did know, what Dorothy through her drunken outburst had made disastrously plain, was that he had been both right and wrong about Buchanan. He had been wrong in thinking him capable of rape, right in thinking him—or being tempted to think him—impotent, and a sexual sadist besides. He had heard the latter from Shelby, and, although tempted by it, had ended by rejecting it—as he had rejected almost the whole of Shelby's story—because it had seemed too pat, too much of a cliché to be true. But now that he had just had the experience of seeing a cliché not merely come true but proceed practically to undress before his eyes, he had to admit the possibility— however tiresome it might seem—that Shelby had been right, that things often *were* pretty much what they appeared to be. Buchanan very probably *had* once deserted his Edenic origins and with them his manhood, even if, in so doing, he had been guilty of the most flagrant breach of originality since the Fall of Adam. Having arrived at this perception, having been in-

structed, even shocked out of his wits by the process of arriving at it, Waithe clung to it with the fanatical determination
of a holy man who, after prolonged mortification of the flesh,
has had revealed to him the primal secret of life. Not only was
it the most convenient summation of what he had come to
know, but it beautifully suited the natural bent of his mind,
for his powers of understanding were such that they operated
best, and perhaps only, when he could take it for granted that
things were pretty much what they appeared to be.

But then he saw that Dorothy had begun to cry. Standing
in the middle of the room holding her breast like a little girl
nursing a cut finger, Dorothy had begun to cry wretchedly and
bitterly, as though at last having rid herself of her insane need
for public vengeance, she had been suddenly overcome by an
awareness of the private wrong she had needed to avenge—the
grievous fact that she had above all been personally hurt. She
stood there for some moments in sobbing lamentation of this
fact. Then slowly and almost, it seemed, in answer to a will
now separate from and greater than her own, her fury rose up
in her once more. She seemed to shudder and choke and fight
to hold back the violence of it as it came, but at last in spite
of her it exploded like retching sickness into hysterics, and she
turned again to Buchanan and screamed out at him in all the
agony of her need, **LOOK** *at me, Buchanan. Look at* **ME.** *See,
it's* **ME** *here. I'm* **REAL,** *I'm* **ALIVE.** *I'm* **HUMAN. GOD-
DAMN YOU.** *See* **ME.** *See* **MEEEEEEEEE.**

It was not until then that Buchanan moved. He moved, in
fact, with such incredible suddenness and swiftness that Waithe
in his confusion was aware of the movement only subconsciously, and stood without quite seeing as Buchanan, with a

heavy, almost leisurely underwater motion, drew back his hand and slapped Dorothy hard across the face. In the next instant the whole scene appeared to blur and shiver before Waithe's eyes, and he felt as though he were looking through a submarine periscope just at the moment when it broke above the surface of the sea. Dorothy's tears seemed abruptly to have turned to blood, and there was a sudden great flow of blood, so sudden and great that her entire face seemed to melt and run with it. Then it was running down her neck and onto her exposed breast and spreading in a dark wet stain over the front of her dress. She appeared to be sobbing out immense tears of blood. But no sound of any kind came from her. She just stood there like a stone figure bleeding by black magic, her eyes wide open and fixed on Buchanan, her naked breast heaving up and down as she breathed and bled, little drops of blood falling rapidly from its injured tip. And no sound at all came from anyone. It was as if all the people in the room had abdicated life in order to live it vicariously through the hypnotic action of her breathing and bleeding. No one made a sound, and no one made a move to help her. She was as alone in her breathing and bleeding as a dying driver hemorrhaging out his lungs in a smashed car in the middle of the Mojave Desert.

In that brief instant of recognized aloneness Dorothy became for the first time completely real to Waithe. It was almost as though her appeal had been addressed to him rather than to Buchanan, and had as inexplicably succeeded with him as, with far better reason, it could only have failed with Buchanan. Yet Waithe knew that the fact of its success with him was not altogether inexplicable. It was due at least in part to the flaw he had just detected in his powers of understanding, the flaw that had driven him to cling with a determination hitherto unknown to him to the reality contained in the appearances of things. It was because he had detected that flaw and been disturbed by it that his abiding fear of cliché had at least for the moment fallen away, and Dorothy was suddenly and for the first time revealed to him, in all her agony and pathos, as the living, suffering woman she had begged Buchanan to be taken for. That, at any rate, was the appearance she gave. That, moreover, was the reality which Waithe, in his new commitment to appearance, should have been perfectly content to receive. Dorothy had materialized before him at the very climax of the anxious séance he had been holding with himself, a creature no longer ghost but fully fleshed and formed, and that ought ideally to have been enough. It was a distinct gain in the direction of both humanity and simple human decency, and, as Shelby might have said, it *felt* true, just as unquestionably it *looked* real.

Yet somehow it was not enough. There was something else, something that Waithe could not quite catch hold of and put a name to about the very appearance that Dorothy gave, and that he had been so eager to accept at face value. Then he thought he knew what it was; he thought he knew even at the expense of sacrificing his newly won belief in the appearances of things, even if it meant descending once again into that abyss of shadows where appearance and reality were almost never, or only by the wildest chance, the same. There had been, he now saw, something very wrong with Dorothy's performance from start to finish. It had all been much too strenuously done, too heavily laid on with a melodramatic trowel, too drenched with tears (and blood), too loud with lamentation, too fraught with cries of torment and the grieved wringing of hands. The intensity of the displayed suffering, the anguish of the public appeal, had been far in excess of the image Dorothy had created of simply a bitterly wronged woman. It was not so much that the emotion behind the performance had been insincere. That, Waithe was certain, had been entirely sincere if anything was. It was more that the emotion had been too powerful to have been logically aroused by the stated facts. Dorothy had grossly overplayed the role of wronged woman; she had been, in respect to that role, a worse ham even than Buchanan customarily was. The intensity of her emotion suggested with absolute conviction a role she had rather decidedly not *appeared* to play. But it was the only role her emotion seemed to fit and to which, since the beginning of time, it had naturally belonged. And that was no more nor less than the role of a woman who could only be in love, and who had been driven to desperation because for some reason her love had not been acknowledged or returned. Dorothy then—however fantastic it might seem—was *in love* with Buchanan, wretchedly and hopelessly in love, and with that remarkable perception the whole crazy jumble of the evening's events fell into order in Waithe's mind like the pieces of a jigsaw puzzle manipulated by remote control.

If Dorothy actually was in love with Buchanan, those events were open to by far the most sensible interpretation Waithe had yet been able to make of them. The thought of Dorothy as a woman capable of *feeling* rather than merely of *making* love had never before occurred to him, but the thought of her as a woman fundamentally *in*capable of telling the truth very definitely had, and he now saw that her whole performance had been a lie. She had lied, it was true, with a conviction born of lifelong practice, but because of the great intensity of her need to lie, she had lied not wisely but too well, so well in fact that she had utterly given herself away. Yet it was just that intensity that helped to vindicate her performance. She had lied, after all, *because* she was a woman in love and, it would seem, a woman scorned besides. If Waithe's calculations were correct, she had not, as she had alleged, been sadistically tortured by Buchanan, nor had she been, as Waithe himself had first supposed, drunkenly raped by him. The evidence now pointed to the far more logical, if altogether bizarre conclusion that Buchanan had simply taken her healthily to bed, but taken her with such manful dexterity and force that his passion had left its mark upon her breast, just as his howl of passion had left its mark upon her mind. It followed, furthermore, that Dorothy had been so profoundly impressed and—perhaps for the first time in her life —so completely awakened by the experience that she had at once fallen desperately in love with him, and had, in her sudden show of outrage, been merely resorting to an extreme variant of the age-old feminine means of punishing him for his subsequent neglect of her. For he had—if all this was indeed the case—to every outward appearance grossly neglected her. He had acted quite simply as if nothing whatever had occurred between them, and that, no less than Dorothy's own secretiveness, had led Waithe to his very first conclusion that —except for the possibility of rape—nothing perhaps had. Still, he had to admit that, regardless of the degree of provocation, her methods *had* been extreme, although they did have a certain queer psychological justification, the superb obviousness of which Waithe could not help but admire. In denouncing Buchanan as she had done, she had been trying to impugn the integrity of the very thing she wanted most—his sex—and positively daring it in the most provocative terms she could think of to prove her wrong by showing its strength to her again. It had, after all, been given to her once and then forever after mysteriously withheld, and, in the face of this fact, she had done the natural, self-flattering thing: she had twisted it into an admission of weakness on Buchanan's part, a sign that he no longer felt capable of doing what he had once done. Or at least in the agony of her frustration she had let herself *appear* to believe it was weakness; she had even played it up to the audience as perversion; for more than anything she wanted to break through to him, kick him in the very groin of his unforgivable, because now unavailable, power over her, even if it meant misrepresenting that power as some kind of sadistic impotence.

It was also possible that she had been trying, by means of this sort of public shock-therapy, to force Buchanan at whatever cost to recognize her as a woman and, therefore, himself as a man. That she had come perilously close to succeeding in the attempt became obvious when one considered that Buchanan had slapped her only *after* she had begun hysterically to insist upon her identity, her humanness, and not when she had far more offensively denounced him as impotent and a fraud. He had acted in this respect very much as Lester Fleischmann had acted that night at the station. When the situation had seemed on the point of making a direct personal claim upon him, a claim far more threateningly personal than any slanderous charge, when, in fact, it had seemed to demand no less than that he *become* a person with a person's inescapable commitment to the real, Buchanan had also in his own fashion gone berserk and taken refuge in violence. In that sense at least Dorothy had succeeded in arousing a response in him.

But it was a response strictly in keeping with his character, and a sign not that he had been goaded into becoming something different from what he was, but rather that he had been frightened into defending what he was. For his slap was only a more muscular form of his gigantic howl, another of his ways of fending off the attentions of the trespassing world and of keeping laboratory pure the vacuum of his immense conceit.

Yet Waithe at least had been forced, if Buchanan had not, to recognize Dorothy as a woman, and also for the first time to recognize Buchanan as a man far different from the one he had formerly appeared to be. Once again it seemed that he had been wrong about them both, as ridiculously wrong as Shelby had been about Buchanan. For if Dorothy was a woman, and a woman capable of love besides, then Buchanan, for all his conceit, was just as surely a man, and a man capable not only of sex but at least of arousing, if not returning, love. The Buchanan whom Shelby had seen was—as Waithe had in the beginning suspected—no more than a creation of his own wishfully thinking mind, a fantasy figure compounded out of nostalgia and sociological moonshine to satisfy a certain need, or compensate for a certain deficiency, in his own nature. For Shelby had also in his fashion fallen in love with Buchanan, and had been unable to live with the simple, unadorned fact of that love's failure. He had had to embellish it, dramatize it, fire it up in the crucible of his transforming imagination, until the responsibility for it seemed to extend into the emotional breakdown of a whole culture, the failure of love in a whole disintegrated way of life. And so he had created the myth of the lost Eden and the forsaken manhood, positively forged it in the white heat of his desperate will to believe. The myth was his way of trying to justify to himself what had happened to Buchanan, and its virtue was the virtue of all myths ever told around the campfires of man's fear of the dark: it depersonalized the hero and changed his defeat into the triumph of overwhelming cosmic odds. Or in this case, since Shelby was a man of his time, it depersonalized Buchanan's infidelity and changed it into a symptom of the prevailing sickness of the age. And Waithe, too, had had his little adventure in myth-making. He had created the myth of Dorothy as he had wanted and needed her to be. In answer to the demands of his own nature, he had quite literally forged her identity as a casually promiscuous, mechanically operated sex machine. And he had done this, he now realized, so that he would not have to confront, and perhaps redeem, the truth of the past he had once shared with her. That past was in a sense *his* lost Eden, as Shelby's past with Buchanan had been his, and he had not wanted any more than Shelby had—or than any campfire sitter ever had—to take up the burden of the past, risk again the perils of humanity, and be forced to face alone in the dark the awful responsibility of at last *becoming* himself a person.

Realizing all this and seeing Dorothy there before him as a woman who seemed, at least in his eyes, to have become a person, Waithe was beset by deeply equivocal feelings and impulses. Now at last and quite alone in the dark he actually was confronted, as by a beast in the jungle, with the inescapable fact of the human, and he did not know what to think or do, whether to run and hide or stand somehow and brave out the challenge which it clearly represented. It was in a way the supreme cliché of all, the final curtain scene in the tired old drama of the absurd which he had sat through so many,

many times before. To have come so far only to find one's self face to face in the end with *this:* the ultimately fatuous, irreducibly fatuous bad joke of just plain everyday reality. It was a joke so wretchedly bad that not even Miriam Hornblower, with all her talent for making bad jokes worse, could have done anything with it. Yet seeing it now in all its abject and shopworn predictability, Waithe was obliged to admit that, perhaps because of its very triteness, it had about it a quality that was almost compelling—like an especially banal "B" picture that, in spite of all one's principles, left one at the end sobbing into one's handkerchief or with heart pumping as fiercely with patriotic pride as any American Legionnaire's. There was a truth in it that Waithe had never before allowed himself to perceive or acknowledge. It was a cliché, to be sure, the very worst of clichés, but when one came down to it, all life was. It had inevitably become so through the treatment given it by so many bad performers in the past. But the raw material had remained unchanged; it was just that Waithe had consistently mistaken the treatment for the material. And with the unchanging material one could always work, make one's own treatment, if one saw it as one's material and saw also how it might be given fresh meaning. It was obvious that in his extravagant, even psychopathic sensitivity to cliché, he had missed something basic, that, in fact, there was almost nothing he had not missed. Reality had all along been *there* to be seen, if only he had been able to bring himself to see it. But he had, ironically enough, learned his lesson too well from Buchanan, from the subtle reprimanding influence which, he realized now, Buchanan had always insidiously exerted upon him. His hatred of cliché he had got from Buchanan—perhaps had even *asked* to get out of some fear of not pleasing or impressing Buchanan—and he had learned the lesson of that fear so well that he had failed altogether to see him or Dorothy or the others or even himself as above all the human and living creatures they were.

About Buchanan there was probably nothing at this late date to be done, but about Dorothy there might still be something. And with that in mind—the vague hope of there being something yet retrievable from the ruin—Waithe took a single step toward her, not knowing what he intended, but knowing more surely than he had ever before known anything in his life that he intended something. In a moment he might perhaps have managed a second step and gone to her and spoken some word or even perhaps have taken her in his arms. But almost before the thought had time to form in his mind, and he felt himself warm to the possibility, he saw that for that also it was much too late. In the middle of his hesitation someone else had come forward to help her, and was now holding a towel up to her face and leading her away. The moment, for whatever potentially it had been worth, had passed him by, eluded him once again, and he was left standing, as she had been left standing, quite alone and helpless, while the impulse to do anything at all died slowly out inside him.

Almost in an effort to punish Dorothy as well as himself for the death of that impulse, Waithe then began to suspect that Buchanan's slap had after all had its queer justification. For, however understandable her motives may have been, Dorothy had still been about to do something very shameful. She had come dangerously close to destroying the communal illusion which held them all together and gave their lives such form and purpose as they had. The fact that she had failed could not be attributed to any flaw in her strategy or her determination, but rather to the superior determination of the people of Cranton to go on believing, regardless of the pressure put upon them, only what they chose to believe. Still, she had almost succeeded by the sheer violence of her attack in forcing them to believe what *she* chose. There had been a moment when even their determination had seemed about to crumble, and the awful reality of her anguish to overcome them with its insupportable weight of truth. It was not merely the fate of the illusion they shared about Buchanan which had at that moment hung so perilously in the balance. It was the fate as well of Buchanan's own illusion about his importance and security in their world. That illusion had also been painfully won, far more painfully even than theirs. If Shelby's story could still be believed at all, it had cost Buchanan no less than his life; it was the thing finally which he had sold out his life for; and the fact that he must surely exist now in bitter daily consciousness of just how poor a bargain he had made only served to enhance the shamefulness of what Dorothy had been about to do. His illusion was all he had left now of a sustaining center of belief, just as it was the nucleus on which the others depended to keep them revolving safely in their own orbits of belief. And in a certain sense Waithe depended on it, too. It was also *his* illusion insofar as he accepted it as a condition of the life he shared with the others and saw, as he was beginning now to see, that his own condition, particularly with respect to Buchanan's influence, was almost inseparable from theirs. It was not something, therefore, to be abandoned lightly, or simply for the sake of a hysterical woman's insistence upon the real. For the country of the real lay, after all, far out beyond the protective circle of the campfire's glow. It was a country of shadows and unknown lurking perils and strange nightmare creatures who sprang out at one unawares and tried to frighten one into becoming something one did not want or dare to be. The journey there was very long and difficult, and Waithe had himself gone only part of the way. But he had learned enough to know that, at least for the world to which he now realized he belonged, even a slap in the face or a gigantic howl was sometimes better and wiser than making that journey and running the risk of confronting alone in the dark the final devastating truth of things as they really were.

6.

So it was that Waithe found himself incredibly pledging at least tentative allegiance to all that he had formerly despised, and so it was too that, much later that night, he found himself even more incredibly standing with Buchanan and of all people—Sylvia on the bank of Cranton River just below the point where the little cluster of Negro shanties kept up their brave show of picturesque squalor before the world. After her bleeding face had been ministered to, Dorothy had disappeared; the party had simply gone on as if nothing whatever had happened; and everyone had become rather drunk. When at last the time came to leave, Waithe had offered to drive Buchanan home; Sylvia—who, following Dorothy's outburst, had attached herself to Buchanan as though aching to be the next to get slapped—had come along uninvited; and on the way Buchanan had suddenly remarked that on such a beautiful moonlit night they positively had to go wading in the river. Since Cranton River was about as suitable for wading as the sewers of Paris, Waithe had assumed that Buchanan was not serious and had, accordingly, said nothing. But Buchanan had proven to be not only serious but resolute. He had demanded that his wishes be carried out immediately, and since he was much too drunk to be reasoned with—and if he had not been, would only have found ways to be even more unreasonable—Waithe decided that it would be better not to argue. Sylvia obviously thought the whole thing was a wonderful idea and the chance of a lifetime really to get *in* with this magnificent man who had not only status but a deliciously perverse habit of hurting women. During the drive to the river she therefore devoted herself to being clever and gay and what she imagined to be provocative, and all the while her big starey eyes gleamed with a gruesome anticipatory light.

When they got out of the car at the riverside, the moon was shining peacefully on the water, and they could hear, coming from the cabins above them, some sort of heavily sentimental, sad-old-darky singing, accompanied by the deep melancholy sound of guitars. Buchanan at once joined in the song and went weaving off up the riverbank, giving out great gusts of boozy baritone and staggering happily about in the undergrowth. When finally he returned, he was carrying a large and weedy bouquet of wild flowers which he presented with an elaborate display of mock gallantry to Sylvia. She accepted it with an equally elaborate, although somewhat less practiced display of mock femininity and favored him with one of her fangy, Hound-of-the-Baskervilles grins. Then, clasping the bouquet like a sick child to her breast, she kicked off her shoes and began tripping gracelessly up and down the bank, flinging the flowers one by one into the air, and giggling as though mad. Buchanan at once pulled off his shoes and socks and started off in guffawing pursuit of her, and for some time they chased each other round and round, in and out among trees and bushes, while Waithe pensively inhaled the stench of garbage and watched several foul-looking objects float sluggishly past the ribbon of moonlight that lay across the water. After a considerable while and a good many shrieks and howls from the shrubbery, Buchanan and Sylvia reappeared, panting and laughing and hanging onto each other, and proceeded down the bank and into the water. Buchanan pushed Sylvia on in ahead of him, and while she made shrill shuddering noises over the cold, he stood for a moment knee-deep in the water and silently surveyed the river, the moon overhead, and the pale surrounding darkness. Then, solemnly adjusting the paper crown which by some miracle still sat on his head, he raised his hand, slowly drew the sign of the cross in the air before him, took a deep breath, and shouted out in a great booming voice, *In the destructive element IMMERSE, in the DE-STRUC-TIVE EL-EE-MENT IMM-ERRRRRSE.* While the night still echoed with the sound, he turned to Waithe, and with a look of incredible slyness, suddenly and mysteriously *winked* at him.

In a single sickening rush of awareness the awful realization of what that wink could only imply swept over Waithe, and he felt he knew at last that he had finally and completely and beyond all redemption been taken in. For with that immemorial gesture of conspiracy Buchanan seemed to have acknowledged—as emphatically as if he had spoken—the existence of some secret understanding or joke which they shared together, and so far as Waithe knew, that could mean only one thing: that Buchanan had somehow sensed what Waithe had imagined that evening to be the truth of his relationship with Dorothy, and was now quite simply and brazenly telling him that he had been foolishly wrong. In that case, everything that Dorothy had said during her hysterical outburst had been true, after all; things in fact *were* as they had initially appeared to be. And Waithe had been tricked by his distrust of the obvious into digging deeper until he had proved, or thought he had proved, with a subtler set of appearances that they were not. But it was now evident that they really were. Dorothy had been *right* in her fantastic account of what had happened on that first fatal night. She *had* been sadistically tortured by Buchanan, and Buchanan actually *was* impotent and a fraud. And now he had the nerve to let Waithe in on the whole sordid secret. He could not resist letting him in, for that was the kind of thing he liked most to do—to badger and torment people with his enigmatic little games while he stood admiring himself before the bottomless mirror of his insufferable conceit.

But then Buchanan shouted a second time, and Waithe realized that he could just as easily be—and at this point very probably was—all wrong about this, too. He saw with an acute sense of his complete helplessness that he could place just as much trust in the believing as in the skeptical side of his nature, and as readily give the one supremacy over him as he could the other. That was the curse of his doubleness of vision, but it might also be—at least in this instance—the blessing. For it enabled him to see that standing side by side with the possible significance of Buchanan's wink was the equally possible significance of the phrase he had shouted. Oddly enough, it was the same phrase that Shelby had once used in describing Buchanan's struggle to remain creatively alive after the death of the movement on which his first work as a poet had been formed. Conrad's Stein had been the original author of the phrase and had tried, in his halting, incoherent way, to affirm through it the fundamental need in everyone to submit to the human condition, to give up the self to life, the necessarily destructive but also ultimately rejuvenating element of perpetual becoming and rebirth. It was quite possible—since now almost anything was—that Buchanan had been using it in the same sense to tell Waithe something which he himself had learned from his own experience, but which Waithe had not, and now undoubtedly never would. It might have been Buchanan's abstruse way of saying that there had to be some point where one plunged deep into the current of life, accepted the risks of one's humanity, or died. And it was very possible that Buchanan had himself already passed that point and might even now be coming back from the other side like some ancient hero-god who, having descended into the underworld, withstood its perils, and been resurrected, had returned to earth with the wisdom forever after simply to *be* what he was. In terms of this idea, Waithe could see that all his speculations about what Buchanan appeared or did not appear to be were entirely irrelevant. However he appeared—whether in the role of impotent, fraud, failure, or in any of his other more deliberate disguises—the important thing was that he had accepted and made some sort of peace with himself. He at least *knew* what he was, even if no one else did. That was the fascinating power which the young wives felt in him and, rightly or wrongly, took for sex. That was the simple strength which had continued to fascinate Waithe even at those times when he had been most annoyingly conscious of its possible falsity.

One had sooner or later to leave off speculating about the nature of reality and become one's self real.

But even as the idea yielded up to him its tantalizing possibilities, Waithe knew, just as he had known when he had taken that single tentative step toward Dorothy, that, as far as he was concerned, it was too late for that also. He was committed finally and forever to what *he* was and would always be—to *his* inescapable reality as a witness and passive watcher at the spectacle of life. He knew as well—and he took his usual pleasure in the knowledge—that this latest ratifying image of Buchanan could very easily be no more than a recurrence in a new form of his old intellectual complaint, his pathetic desire to believe, despite all his skepticism, in something, and his weakness for imagining, when he could not find, something in which to believe. In the light of this realization the figure of Buchanan in the guise of some kind of fertility god or martyred saint stood before him in all its mocking triteness, positively daring him to go on and make an even bigger fool of himself. For it was a figure which again Waithe had created out of the need to satisfy the impotent requirements of his own nature. And what was far worse, the significance of the phrase which had led him to create this figure came from the same place where Buchanan—and Shelby before him—had got the phrase itself—not from life, or any speculations upon life, but from the reading of books, the source, it now seemed, of all Waithe's significances, and very nearly all the experiences he appeared capable of having.

7.

So at last it was that, in his now accepted role of untrust-worthy witness, Waithe turned once again to face the spec-tacle of life before him. From the Negro shanties, seemingly so secure in their little world of sentimental illusion, the sad sound of singing mingled with the soft thrum of guitars still drifted over the river like a doleful lamentation for the dead. Gray wisps of cloud were beginning to move across the moon, and in the diminished light Waithe could just see the figures of Buchanan and Sylvia as they waded slowly away from him through the shallow water. Sylvia had pulled her skirt above her hips and was still holding the last of her bouquet of flow-ers. Buchanan waded somewhat unsteadily beside her, mutter-ing and singing to himself. In the pale semidarkness they ap-peared to be moving through thick layers of primeval mist, and for a moment they seemed to Waithe like figures rising up out of the watery beginnings of the world, first man and first woman spontaneously spawned in a river as yet unfouled by time and history, still flowing cleanly and proudly, sparklingly cold and alive with fish. But then, with the sudden movement of a cloud, the illusion vanished; the whole scene was illumi-nated by a ghostly white light; and Sylvia with a shrill cry threw her flowers high in the air, then held out her arms to catch them as they fell. But they scattered beyond and around her on the dark water and gradually drifted away past the twisted shape of a huge tree lying half buried in the mud, and joined a few eggshells that bobbed along on the surface and some broken orange crates and bits of wood. Then the moon darkened again, and Buchanan and Sylvia once more became shadowy and indistinct to Waithe, until he could see only the vague flash now and then of Sylvia's thin white thighs. The river's slow current moved placidly past him as he stood there and peered into the darkness, the river's slow current bearing its little flotillas of refuse and scum steadily and with a certain chuckling joy forever on through time and out to sea. And Buchanan and Sylvia kept moving with it steadily away from Waithe, until at last they faded altogether into the darkness, and he was left, baffled to the end, watching over nothing.

Munich 1958–59